PRESUMED GUILTY

PRESUMED GUILTY

A NOVEL

ALEXANDRA SHAPIRO

NEW DEGREE PRESS

PRESUMED GUILTY

A Novel

ISBN   978-1-63730-640-6   *Paperback*

            978-1-63730-724-3   *Kindle Ebook*

            978-1-63730-915-5   *Ebook*

"With great power there must also come—great responsibility."

"The citizen's safety lies in the prosecutor who tempers zeal with human kindness, who seeks truth and not victims, who serves the law and not factional purposes, and who approaches his task with humility."

CONTENTS

In memory of Ian Yankwitt.

***

To Matthew, Emily, and Andrew, my three shining stars, and to Jonathan, who helped me learn how to think like a defense lawyer.

PART ONE

THE "CRIME"

CHAPTER 1

A DAY IN THE LIFE OF EMMA SIMPSON

MARCH 14, 2012

PITCHER LANE, RED HOOK, NEW YORK

Wednesday, March 14, was just like many other workdays. Emma was rudely awakened at 4:30 a.m. by the sounds of Pink Floyd's "Another Brick in the Wall" blaring out of her alarm clock. She rolled over and quickly tapped the off button, hoping not to wake up Pierre. He could sleep through anything, though, and was sound as a rock. She took a quick look at his fire-red hair, smiled, and then scooted off to brush her teeth and get ready for the day.

Emma felt a little more sluggish than usual as she began her insane weekday routine. Quick shower, grab coffee, water bottle, Greek yogurt and a banana, head out the door, and drive the ten minutes to catch the 5:15 a.m. train from Rhinecliff to Penn Station so she could be at her desk in midtown Manhattan at around 7:30 a.m. The coffee was *key*, especially today. She reached the kitchen just as the freshly ground dark French roast finished brewing and inhaled its rich, deep aroma, which always reminded her of her mom. When she was growing up, her mom, a huge Francophile, always insisted that no one in the family should deign to drink the typical "American" coffee that everyone else drank in the 1970s—ground, mud-brown coffee out of a can. Way before Starbucks and the coffee revolution, her mother insisted on coffee made from dark, rich whole beans, ground fresh every day.

Pouring the coffee into her travel mug, Emma added a splash of foamy milk, watching as it turned the perfect caramel color. She laughed to herself about how in high school, when she woke up at 5:00 a.m. to get to basketball practice, she used to drink it black, like her dad. Fortunately it had dawned on her—after one too many college all-nighters fueled by gallons of the stuff—that it actually tasted pretty bad that way but could be delicious with a splash of milk. And thankfully, every night Pierre would grind the beans, pour the water, and set the coffee maker's timer for her the night before, so it was ready just as she was sneaking out of the house.

Waking up at 4:30 in the morning was far from ideal, but Emma was used to the routine. The morning train ride provided much-needed "quiet time" to read the news, catch up on email and get ready for the day. And it was a scenic train ride. For most of the trip, the tracks hugged the Hudson River. Emma always sat by the window, so she could take in the small boats, the transition in color as the sun rose, and the seasonal changes in the foliage. It was a soothing prelude to the cacophony of the office, and on the way home sometimes you could catch a pretty sunset.

Emma grew up in Manhattan and thrived on the city and its energy, but she also loved the outdoors and wanted her kids to grow up hiking, biking, and playing outside. When her oldest child, Daniel, was about five, she and Pierre bought a small weekend house in the Hudson Valley, in Red Hook, New York. It provided a perfect escape from the hustle and bustle; you could feel the stress dissipating like the air out of a popped balloon every time the car crossed the Henry Hudson Bridge on Friday nights. A couple of years later, they found a farm and decided to move the family there for good. The biggest challenge was Emma's long commute. She spent around four hours a day traveling back and forth most weekdays.

Emma managed the New York office of Otis Capital, the hedge fund she'd worked at for the past ten years. When she got the big job last year, she had mixed emotions. Of course, she was excited about her new role and a little surprised that she'd somehow managed to surpass all the brown-nosing self-promoters she'd encountered along the way. But sometimes she was racked with self-doubt. Was she really up to the job? Had they chosen her *because* she was a woman, for the public relations kudos?

And then there were the bigger questions. Was this what she should be doing with her life? She had always been a striver, working to get this brass ring and the next—the fancy college and graduate school, the academic honors, the job at Goldman Sachs early on, and now this. But ever since Daniel was born, and then Sarah, these achievements seemed more like window dressing. Yes, they helped keep everyone more than comfortable and anchored the family, but at what cost? Sometimes Emma wished she could hit the pause button, get off the treadmill, and take stock, perhaps find another path. Maybe when she turned fifty and had saved up enough money, she'd finally have the guts to do it.

On this day, though, Emma had to focus on the here and now—her immediate challenges and not grand (or maybe grandiose) questions of deeper purpose. She got on the train, found her usual seat, and nodded to the couple of regular passengers seated in the sparsely populated car. It was dark outside and very quiet except for the rhythmic *clink, clink, clink* of the train moving along the tracks.

Emma started going through emails received since last night and working on responses to things she had not gotten to the day before. She spent most of the commute reviewing and responding to all the messages that had piled up in her inbox and perusing the *Wall Street Journal*, the *Financial Times*, and analyst reports about various companies her group had invested in or were considering for new investments. By the time the train pulled into Penn Station and she embarked on the short walk to the office, Emma was ready to start her workday.

* * *

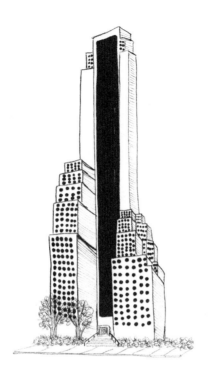

500 FIFTH AVENUE, NEW YORK, NEW YORK

"Morning," Emma greeted the guard in the early-twentieth-century art deco skyscraper as she waved her swipe card over the scanner at the gate. The doors thwacked open, and she headed to the elevator. At least she didn't have to deal with those awkward interactions one sometimes had with other passengers since today no one was inside the car. She glanced at the captivate screen, which flashed recent NBA scores. The Knicks lost, yet again. As usual they had virtually no chance of a playoff run, so Emma hadn't been following them much this season. The elevator stopped on forty-five, and Emma headed out and through the double glass doors into Otis's offices.

The receptionist wasn't in yet, and things were still quiet. Emma headed to her corner office and glanced out the south window, taking in the morning view of Bryant Park and the Empire State Building. It was too cloudy today, but sometimes you could see the Statue of Liberty in the distance.

She skirted around the sleek granite L-shaped desk she had personally designed for the space and turned on her computer and monitors. While she waited for them to boot up, her eyes rested on the large still life of pears her best friend from elementary school had painted. She liked it because it added a touch of color to the space but reflected a classic, simple taste unlikely to offend potential investors. Much like the photos of Pierre and the kids from their travels or sports events scattered around her office, which gave her comfort and helped ease her anxiety during stressful moments at work.

Emma glanced at her calendar today, groaning at the back-to-back meetings. She spent the quiet time before the first meeting reviewing slides she would present at her 9:00 a.m. meeting and the preliminary March data colleagues from the other offices had sent about fund performance and positions. That meeting was uneventful.

At 10:00 a.m., Emma headed into the conference room for the New York meeting, where folks were slowly congregating and grabbing coffee. "Hey, Ben, what's up? Is Doug here yet?"

Ben Noguchi was Emma's top lieutenant and best friend at Otis. "I haven't seen Doug yet," he said. He sipped his coffee and groaned as he took the seat next to hers. "I'm exhausted. Rachel's with me this week, and she insisted on staying up until midnight to watch *Harry Potter and the*

Order of the Phoenix for, like, the tenth time. It's amazing the way these kids can watch the same movie over and over." Ben rolled his eyes.

"Well, at least she's not spending hours and hours glued to a screen playing video games and blowing off her homework. If it wasn't for basketball, who knows if Daniel would ever leave the house on weekends," Emma said.

"Oh hey, there he is." Ben looked toward the door. "Morning, Doug."

"How y'all doing?" Doug Jones, the New York legal and compliance guy, responded in his Alabama twang. The rest of them filed in.

"Let's get started," said Emma. "Ben, can you give us an update on where we are with the transition to the new server and other upgrades to the computer system? Just a quick synopsis of timing and how we're trying to minimize any disruption while the upgrades are implemented."

After Ben summarized the anticipated changes and when they would be rolled out, Emma went down her list of companies the funds had positions in, and the analysts ran through the latest data, rumors, and market scuttlebutt they had picked up about each company. A couple of the funds were considering positions in some small pharma companies that were currently running clinical trials on potentially promising treatments for Alzheimer's and other forms of dementia.

"PLP has some new doctors on board. It might be useful to see if any of them can help us to figure out which of these drugs has the best chance," Ben pointed out. "I'll send you guys the bios."

"Ben, we need to be careful about PLP. They've given us some good experts, but the recent witch hunt by the US Attorney has me a little concerned," Doug interjected. "Some of these 'experts' are really just selling inside information, and there's nothing Peter Weisman loves more than taking down hedge funds and getting himself on national magazine covers. We don't want to be on Weisman's radar if we can help it. So let's discuss who these doctors are before we sign any of them up. We need to make sure they're legit and that none of them are involved in any of the clinical studies."

"For sure, of course," Ben relented. "I'll send you the names first."

"Thanks. Hopefully there's no issue, but you can't be too careful these days," warned Doug. "The Boston office, in fact, apparently just heard that one of their expert consultants got a subpoena related to some investigation into Delphun Media trades. I don't know the details, but the media and entertainment team up there had been using a consultant through another firm—not PLP—and it turned out the guy may have been working for Delphun. Keep that in the cone, though. We can't have everyone in the firm blabbing about this thing."

Doug glanced at the analysts. Then he sucked his lips into his mouth and gave Emma a look. *What was that about?* Emma wondered. *Maybe he feels like he shouldn't have said so much about this Delphun issue?*

It was almost 11:00 a.m. Emma glanced at her agenda to make sure they'd covered all the topics she needed to hit and saw one more item on the list. "We only have a few more minutes, but I think we need to start thinking about some cryptocurrency investments. Who wants to put together—"

"Isn't crypto way too volatile and risky for us?" Marshall Minnow, who managed the energy portfolio and seemed like he was already in the industry when Emma was born, interrupted. The corners of his mouth crimped upward. "It could all crash any time. It's like the Wild West—totally unregulated. And not the right fit for our investors, who are more cautious."

Stay calm, Emma told herself. He was always interrupting and belittling her, but it was best to ignore it. She was the boss; it was his problem if he couldn't deal with it. She gritted her teeth and gave him a look, waiting to make sure *he* was finished.

Then she said impassively, "Well, there's no harm in doing some research so we can make an informed judgment about whether to get into this new space." She turned to Dylan Morrison, a junior analyst with a computer science degree who seemed to know a lot about crypto. "I'd like to see a white paper on it. Dylan, do you have time?"

"Sure, boss. I think this is a great time to get into it," Dylan said.

Well, at least somebody agrees, Emma thought, shooting a half-smile in Marshall's direction.

"I can put together a draft for you in the next week or two, if that works," Dylan said.

"Great, thanks," Emma replied. "And if you see any interesting items while you're working it up, send them along in the meantime."

The meeting broke up, and Emma headed into her office for her next meeting.

* * *

After reviewing the latest numbers for each New York fund with the Chief Financial Officer, Emma headed out to lunch. Analise Epstein, a friend from college, was already sitting at a table near the staircase at Ammos Estiatorio, the Greek seafood place on Vanderbilt Avenue that Analise liked. Emma waved and then gave her a hug when she got to the table.

"It's been ages," said Analise.

"I know." Emma laughed. She glanced at the menu. "Let's order before we forget." She waved over the waiter.

After they ordered and chatted a bit, Emma told Analise about the winery Pierre had just started.

"This is his life's dream. When we first met, I was studying in Paris. I thought it would just be a fling because why would he ever leave France? He had just opened a small wine store on the left bank, and his idea of 'work' was traveling to the Loire Valley to tour wineries and decide what to buy." Emma sighed wistfully. "But then, you know, he decided to follow me here, and he gave that up and tried to become a corporate lawyer. I always felt guilty about that, but he seems much happier now."

"Good for him," Analise said. "How far along is the business?"

"Well, it's still early days. For now, he's buying harvested grapes from other vintners so he can get some product out, but he also planted some grapes. Eventually he's hoping to grow most of his own crop." She went on to describe the two types of wine and how the cellar would be opening for tours and tastings this summer.

"I'm definitely in. I've always wanted to get into the wine business," Analise said. "Plus, I'd love to check out the little store, and we are thinking of renting a place in Dutchess County this summer anyway. When can we come up to get the tour?"

It was almost 1:30 p.m. by then. "Whenever you like. Just let me know when you guys have a free weekend." Emma glanced at her watch. "Listen, I need to head back for a two o'clock meeting. Can we get the check?"

A few moments later, Emma was on her way back to the office. Back at her desk, she perused the bios of two prospective investors. Richard Ginsberg, the Chief Executive Officer of Otis, set up the meeting with some family office guys who seemed to have lots of cash to burn. Richard thought they were looking to invest up to five million dollars in Otis health care funds. Richard was "working" from his home in Jackson, Wyoming, and joining by phone.

Emma would be the only woman at the meeting, but that was par for the course. At this point, she hardly noticed. Things had changed a lot since she was one of the few girls in the advanced math classes in high school. She'd almost given up on them in eleventh grade, when her math teacher kept ignoring her to call on boys. But her dad insisted she persevere, and she got the last laugh when she won the school's math prize.

The meeting with the investors went smoothly, and it looked like they were going to do the full $5 million. Emma spent the next hour jumping from dozens of emails to phone calls and constantly bouncing from one task to the next. The emails just kept coming, wave after wave of them. She read some of the team's research on whether to try and invest in some new company called "Zoom" that made videoconference software. *I wonder where they got the name*, thought Emma. It reminded her of that kids' TV show on PBS she sometimes watched growing up.

At 3:55 p.m., an alert popped up in the corner of the screen reminding her that at 4:00 p.m., she had to conduct the first of two interviews for entry-level analyst positions. Emma quickly scanned what hit her in box while reviewing the paper on Zoom. There were several from Ben, including one to Emma, her other deputy, Doug, and the portfolio managers. It said something about the computer system upgrade and the importance of clearing out unneeded files to prepare for it.

Emma started reading Ben's email, but then her computer beeped. She took her eyes off the screen, picked up the two résumés, and headed into the glass-paneled conference room.

"Nice to meet you, Alan." Emma extended her hand. The guy had a fish handshake. Not a good sign. *How carefully do they screen these interviewees before wasting my time with them?* Emma wondered. "I'm Emma Simpson, head of our New York office. Did someone offer you something to drink?" She motioned toward the coffee and water bottles on the side table.

"I'm set, thanks." The guy was sweating bullets.

"So, why do you want to be an equities analyst?" Emma asked. He droned on with the usual platitudes. It was so hard to know if these applicants would be any good. Their paper credentials were meaningless.

She tried another tack. "Suppose you've got a buddy whose dad is the CEO of an immunotherapy company that you cover. You know the company is in the middle of a clinical trial for a new cancer treatment. You're out having drinks, and your buddy tells you his dad was in a foul mood last night, yelling at him for no reason and snapping at his fifteen-year-old sister. What do you do with the information?"

The guy looked like a deer in headlights. "Um, well, I guess he didn't say anything about the company, or *why* his dad was upset. So I'd probably recommend we short the stock, since chances are his dad was angry because of a bad development in the drug trial."

All right, this was going nowhere. You'd think he'd at least mention the need to run a tricky issue by legal and compliance. She looked at her watch. The interview was supposed to last thirty minutes and it was only 4:15 p.m., but she wasn't going to waste any more time. "Listen, thanks for coming in. We'll get back to you soon." She ushered him out.

Unfortunately, the next one wasn't much better. They needed to cast a wider net. Too many boring résumés with standard credentials but people who lacked judgment or couldn't think their way out of a paper bag.

It was almost 5:00 p.m., and Emma had to catch the 5:45 p.m. train home. She sent Ben a note nixing the two applicants and telling him to find some outstanding students who majored in humanities instead of all these quant and business majors. And how about some women, for once? Then she read through the rest of the emails she had received during the interviews. There was another missive from Ben about the computer system changes. As she opened it, Emma grimaced. *This is such an enormous pain in the butt. What was wrong with our existing system anyway? It's not as if we do high-frequency trading. I never should have gone along with this.*

The email was to employees in the New York office. The subject was "Upcoming computer system upgrades." The message contained a schedule of what was being rolled out and when, and it warned people about times the old servers would be down during the transition. As she started to scan the remaining paragraphs, Emma's cell phone rang. It was Daniel.

"Mom, I need your help with a computer science problem," he said.

"Listen, little man, I need to head to the train in a few minutes, and anyway, how am I supposed to help you from here? Can you ask your sister or Dad?" Of course, Emma was the one who had studied math and comp sci. And the suggestion that Pierre Elis, who hadn't taken a math class since his high school days in Paris, could help on this one was ludicrous. He knew nothing about coding. Sarah was a whiz, though of course Daniel didn't want to ask his younger sister to help with homework.

"Mom, be serious. I guess I'll wait 'til you get home." Daniel sighed and hung up.

Emma shut down her laptop, grabbed her backpack, put on her jacket, and headed out. "See you tomorrow, Tony," she told the receptionist and made a beeline for the door.

* * *

Emma hustled over to Penn Station and just barely made the 5:45 p.m. Empire train. Her preferred seat on the third car was taken, but she found another window seat and settled in. As she reached into her backpack to retrieve her iPad, she heard a loud voice approaching. She looked across the aisle and saw a man in a business suit yelling at whomever he was talking to on his cellphone.

Emma debated moving, but the train was almost full. Instead, she inserted her EarPods and found her classic rock playlist. The sound of Fleetwood Mac's "Tusk" began wafting into her ears. Emma thumbed through the news and her Twitter feed. Nothing too exciting, so she opened her personal email. A note from the PTA about the spring benefit; a note from Daniel's dean about upcoming parent-teacher conferences; a reminder about sign-up for spring sports teams; and a receipt from the hotel in Big Sky for the rest of the deposit on the family's upcoming ski trip.

Thinking about Big Sky put a smile on Emma's face as she pictured the hot tub in front of the cabin with its view of the snowy slopes. It brought back memories of earlier trips, with the kids laughing as they raced each other down the mogul runs and made fun of her and Pierre for trailing behind.

A text from Daniel popped up in the family group chat. "What's for dinner?"

The daily question. All this kid could think about at the end of the day was food. She responded, "Dad told me he's making lasagna. I should be home by eight-ish. Save some for me if you can't wait."

She returned to her email. Dylan forwarded some reports about cryptocurrencies he was researching. She scanned a couple of them and then did a Google search to see where they were trading.

After reviewing the remaining unread items, Emma remembered Ben's email about getting ready for the new computer system. *When did he say the system would next be down?* She glanced through the schedule, which was followed by this: "As we prepare for the transition to a new server and update our firmwide computer system, we wanted to remind you about Otis's document retention policy." It explained which documents had to be preserved and for how long and attached a copy of the policy. A reference to the importance of discarding research notes about investment ideas and conversations with sources was underlined and bolded.

Seems like a good idea to remind people about the policy, Emma thought as she inserted her cursor above his message and typed: "We know these disruptions to the computer system are frustrating, but these upgrades include important speed enhancements, especially for our trading desk. And it's always a good idea to declutter and make sure everyone is following our document policy. These procedures are designed to protect the firm and its employees in case there is ever a lawsuit or regulatory inquiry. Please talk to a compliance officer if you have any questions." Then she hit send.

Emma glanced at her watch. Half an hour to go. She switched the music to an REM album and pulled out her copy of *Lyndon Johnson: Master of the Senate* by Robert Caro and started reading. Before she knew it, the train was pulling into Rhinecliff. She hopped out, found her car in the parking lot, and drove home.

As she pulled into the driveway, Emma took in the familiar sight of the large, modern, ranch-style house with its big windows that filled the rooms with sunlight when the weather was good. It gave her a calm, peaceful feeling and erased the stress that had built up during her busy day. She loved the open, airy feeling created by the high ceilings and the warmth emanating from the large fireplace in the living room on this cold winter day. It was so comforting and peaceful, after the hurly-burly of the city and the crowds at the train station, to come home to this secluded plot of land next to the old red barn Pierre recently restored. The nearest neighbor's driveway was about a quarter-mile down the road.

Emma noticed that the signs for the fruit and vegetable stand and advertising the lunches served in the barn were still out. She pulled them down and headed toward the house.

Ghost and Dyer ran out to her and started barking at the tops of their lungs. The Siberian Huskies jumped all over her as she tried to walk in the door. "Well, at least someone is happy to see me!"

Everyone was just sitting down to dinner when Emma entered the house. The large round granite table in the kitchen was filled with big plates of pasta and salad, and the air was thick with the scent of freshly baked bread. "Perfect timing, I see," said Pierre. Emma kissed everyone, dumped her things, and sat down.

"How was everyone's day?"

"Good," said Sarah. "You won't believe what happened. Ocean's brother, Larsen, wasn't in school today, and people are saying he was suspended—or maybe even expelled. They said he posted some nasty pictures making fun of girls on the swim team."

"That seems a little extreme. Don't you think?" Pierre asked.

Sarah shrugged her shoulders. "I guess so, but Larsen's kind of a jerk anyway. I hate going to their house when he's home. He creeps me out."

"Well, you guys better be super-careful about this kind of stuff. Don't forget, when you're online lots of people can see what you say. It's not private, and you can get in trouble if someone gets offended," Pierre said. "By the way," he continued, "did you hear that Giuseppe's is going to close? The owner is moving out of town and working on a new business in Tivoli."

"Dad, isn't that good news? Maybe you can open a fancier restaurant now—less competition!" suggested Sarah. Emma laughed.

"Not on your life! I've got my hands full with this winery and the store for now," Pierre responded. "Did you know that ninety percent of restaurants fail in the first year?"

"Dad, how can you think like that? A *real* restaurant would be super-fun. Your cooking is so amazing. Maybe you could even become one of those celebrity chefs!" Sarah said.

Daniel grinned and said, "Yeah, Dad, and what about that show *Chopped*? You could kick ass on that show. Your food would knock their socks off, especially since you're always focused not just on the taste, but also on 'la presentation,' or however you say that."

"And what about *Shark Tank*?" Sarah asked. "Aren't you an entrepreneur? You could get them to invest in the winery, and then that would take off and you could focus on the new restaurant."

Emma poured herself a glass of red wine and smiled at Pierre as the kids continued fantasizing about their father's ascension into fame and glory.

Pierre laughed. "We moved here so you kids could be close to nature, but you seem to spend more time watching TV than anything else. But I gotta admit, it would be pretty cool to be on *Chopped*, and I bet I'd do well. I can get pretty creative with different ingredients."

By this time, everyone's plates were totally empty. Sarah disappeared to her room, supposedly to work on an English paper. Daniel left to work out in the basement after claiming he'd figured out the comp sci assignment and didn't need Emma's help after all.

Emma cleared the table and put the dishes in the dishwasher.

"Shall we go for a walk? " Pierre asked. "It's such a nice evening, finally starting to warm up."

"Why not? Let's take Ghost and Dyer." Emma grabbed their leashes and her jacket and joined Pierre outside.

The night was clear and brisk, and the only sounds were from the crickets and the crunching of their shoes on the road. They could see the Milky Way and a bright light that was probably Venus.

All in all, a pretty good day, Emma thought.

PART TWO

THE INVESTIGATION

CHAPTER 2

THE INVESTIGATION (INSIDER TRADING PHASE)

—

NOVEMBER 20, 2012

ONE SAINT ANDREW'S PLAZA, NEW YORK, NEW YORK

The fluorescent lights cast a sickly greenish glow on the peeling gray paint covering the dingy walls as Annie Waters headed down the hallway outside her office on the fifth floor of the US Attorney's Office in Manhattan. The building was a textbook example of 1970s-era "brutalist" or Soviet-style architecture on the outside. And the inside was even worse—hardly what you might expect for the premier federal prosecutor's office in the country. On her way to Rafael Eduardo "Ted" Hardin's office, Annie walked by the disabled water fountain. She glanced at the "Do Not Drink" sign, which was posted after someone finally figured out that lead from the pipes had been leaching into the water.

Annie peeked into Ted's office. He was at his desk typing, with his back to the open door. His broad shoulders and tight biceps looked like they were bursting out of his blue dress shirt. *Does he buy them too small on purpose to look bigger?* she wondered.

She knocked lightly. He turned around and said, "C'mon in." His eyes lit up like shiny sapphires as he flashed her one of those winsome smiles. Annie was caught off guard for a minute. She paused to collect her train of thought and refocus. Then she walked in and sank into the leather chair across from his desk.

"Ted, I have real reservations about this case. We've been looking into Otis's trading for over a year, but there's no concrete evidence of any insider trading. Unless someone flips or there's some new break in the investigation, I really don't see how we can bring any charges that could stick."

Ted cast a withering look downward from his higher perch behind the bulky wooden desk. "Annie, we can't give up now, after all the work we've done. Otis *must* have gotten inside information on Delphun. The trades are just too good to be true. They short the stock just before earnings are announced. Then, lo and behold, the earnings turn out to be lower than predicted by most analysts and lower than Delphun's guidance. Sometimes they buy the stock just before an announcement, and it turns out earnings were better than expected. They've made millions off these trades. You think they're clairvoyant or just better than other hedge funds because they're smarter?"

He threw down his pen.

"C'mon. When things seem too good to be true, they are. Otis has an illegal edge. They must."

Annie tugged at one of her long frizzy brown curls and sighed. Ted, like everyone else in the Securities Unit, was eager to make a name for himself and put some more scalps on US Attorney Peter Weisman's insider-trading trophy wall. Of course, Annie would love to make the case too. But the evidence was what it was, and it just wasn't there. And maybe they *weren't* insider trading after all.

She said, "The trades do look fishy, but there's no smoking gun. There's no email, no text, no recorded phone call suggesting they got any information from an insider. They have documents that seem to back up the story that they used their own research and public information to make their trading decisions. And we don't have a cooperator." Ted glanced down at his phone, so she tried another tack. "We'd get killed if they took it to trial. It would be Peter's first big loss. We'd be toast in the Office."

"Well, let's go talk to Jared. It's time to fish or cut bait. And who knows, maybe he'll have some idea, something we haven't thought about." Ted stood up and motioned Annie toward the door.

They headed over to see Unit Chief Jared Bosworth and parked themselves on his dirt-brown, faux leather couch. Like the chair in Ted's office, the couch was low to the ground, and the cushion swallowed Annie up. But Ted's six-foot three-inch frame seemed immune to that quicksand effect. Bosworth retrieved a golf ball he'd been putting into a paper cup, placed it on the carpet six feet away from the cup, and tapped it back with his putter. The ball swerved slightly left of the cup, hit his refrigerator, and bounced away.

Ted and Annie reprised their exchange. Ted weighed in first. "Jared, there's no way these guys have beaten the market so many times based on skill or luck. They must have some kind of illegal edge. There are five sets of trades we should charge with total gains of over ten million dollars."

Annie protested. "I just think we're going to have a hard time making it stick. We can't prove they got any inside info. They used some consultants, but it's not clear any of them were insiders. They have all these documents in this internal matrix where they collected analysis. They'll say they did their own projections, and it was all on the up and up."

"What about texts and WhatsApp? Anyone using personal accounts instead of the recorded lines and computers to discuss dirty info? And have you guys checked into whether anyone destroyed any documents?" Jared interrogated Ted and Annie. "Maybe they covered up the evidence."

"We, uh, really haven't seen any offline chats like that," Annie replied. *We haven't focused on that*, she thought. *Have we missed something?* "Either their research was kosher, or they knew how to cover their tracks."

"Well, what about this guy Frances? Have we spoken to him? Doesn't he have a tax problem or something? Maybe we can put some pressure on him and he'll flip." Jared collected the golf ball and put it back to line up another putt.

"I don't know. He's in the New York office. These trades were handled by Boston. He probably doesn't know anything," Annie said.

Ted disagreed. "You know, that's not a bad idea. I think he may have failed to report some big gambling winnings—like a couple hundred thou. Of course, we can't bring tax charges without approval from Washington. But he won't know it's a bluff. And who knows. Maybe he's got other 'issues.' Let's see what dirt we can find on the guy and bring him in."

"Well, I don't know—I think you're barking up the wrong tree," Annie murmured. She felt like she was sinking further and further into the couch. "It's probably a waste of time," she said hesitantly.

"What's the downside? Let's see if he knows something," Ted said. "I'll call Otis's lawyers tomorrow and tell them we want to interview him."

"Good," Jared nodded approvingly. "Peter's eager to do something here, so let's see if we can bring this thing back to life."

This case was like a black hole, and Annie was getting sucked further and further inside it. The exit ramps all seemed to be disappearing. She slowly pulled herself up from the couch and slunk toward the door.

* * *

DECEMBER 15, 2012

ONE SAINT ANDREW'S PLAZA, NEW YORK, NEW YORK

Frances O'Brien emerged from the subway at Brooklyn Bridge-City Hall and turned north toward One Saint Andrew's Plaza. *Shit*, he thought, looking up at the sky. During his twenty-minute ride, the sun had disappeared and rain was pouring out of the ominous charcoal gray clouds now blanketing the sky. He darted across the square toward the white security tent in front of the US Attorney's Office. The rain washed over his gray suit and brand new antique calf-skin Bruno Magli loafers as he dashed inside.

"Can I help you?" barked a security guard imperiously.

Frances's eyes darted around the plaza. Where was Marc Levy, the lawyer Otis hired to represent him? They were supposed to meet outside the tent, but Frances's thousand-dollar shoes would be drenched even more if he waited. "Uh, I'm meeting—"

Just then, a short, stocky man with graying dirty blond hair and blue rectangular glasses entered the tent, retracted his umbrella, and extended his hand. "Hi, Frances." Marc turned to the guard and presented his ID. "He's with me. We're here to see Ted Hardin and Annie Waters."

A few minutes later, the two men were directed into the cavernous lobby at the US Attorney's Office. Marc guided them over to a couple of wooden folding chairs and away from two other visitors, who were conferring in hushed tones. As they waited for the prosecutors to escort them upstairs, Marc turned to Frances and spoke quietly. "Now look, Frances, the most important thing is to tell the truth. Just answer their questions as best you can, and we'll be fine. I don't think they're looking to jam you up; they're investigating some trades in the Boston office. That's why we're here."

Frances glanced around to make sure the other people weren't listening and leaned in toward Marc. "But why do they need me? I wasn't involved in those trades. I don't know where the Boston guys got their info. This whole thing is a waste of time. Are you sure this isn't some kind of trap?" Frances whispered.

"I haven't seen anything in your emails or chats that concerns me. But is there something you're not telling me? If you don't come clean with me, you know, I can't do my job," Marc said.

He fixed his gaze on Frances. "If there's something you wouldn't want on the front page of the *Wall Street Journal* or wouldn't want your mother to find out, you better tell me now. The absolute worst thing that could happen here is if I learn about something bad that you've done for the first time in front of the prosecutors."

"Of course not. I've got nothin' to hide—" Frances lowered his voice as he noticed a tall young man in a tight-fitting suit with a sculptured visage emerge from behind the steel doors and head toward them. *That must be an FBI agent. He's too muscular and good-looking to be a lawyer*, Frances guessed.

"Hey, Marc, how's it going?" The guy gave Marc a bear hug. "Enjoying life on the dark side?" Frances realized that Christopher Reeve here was actually one of the prosecutors. Who would have thought?

"Very funny. Things are good. It's a little more challenging when you have to defend people, you know. At least that's true for me. Remember, when I was in the Office, I prosecuted real bad guys, not these paper cases you love." Marc grinned and motioned toward Frances. "This is Frances O'Brien."

Hardin led them through the steel doors up the elevator to the fifth floor and ushered them into a small, windowless conference room. "Here's the proffer agreement." He put a two-page typed document on the table. "Be right back."

A rectangular mud-colored laminate table dominated the cramped room. The low ceilings were barely lit by long, tubular 1970s era fluorescent lights, though two appeared to have blown out. A large boxy television set—which also looked like it had barely escaped the 1970s—sat at the end of the table. Marc and Frances sat down on a couple of unmatched, old, and worn chairs near the TV.

Marc signed the document and motioned for Frances to do the same. "This is the 'queen for a day' agreement we went over before. The prosecutors will probably explain it, but as I told you, it gives you almost no protection if they ever go after you. They can't use your statements directly against you. But they can use what you say to develop other evidence, cross-examine you, and attack your defense if you're ever charged with a crime. And if they think you've lied, you're toast. You can be prosecuted for false statements," Marc explained. "Understand?"

Frances nodded. It was legal mumbo-jumbo, but it seemed like he didn't have much of a choice, so he signed the document. He heard voices approaching and looked up.

Superman was back, this time with an attractive, petite young woman (sort of a Lois Lane type, in fact). A short baby-faced guy in jeans and a T-shirt who looked about fifteen years old accompanied them. It turned out baby-face was Special Agent Marsh, and Lois was another prosecutor, Annie Waters.

Hardin sat directly across from Frances, flanked by baby-face Marsh on the right and Waters on the left. Neither of the prosecutors had any notes, any writing implements, or any paper. Marsh seemed to be the designated note-taker and only said about two words during the entire two-hour meeting.

Hardin took command. "Thanks for coming in. As you undoubtedly know, we're investigating some suspicious Otis trades. Now, I'm sure your lawyer has told you this, because he's very good at his job, but it's crucial that you understand this. You cannot lie to us. That would be a very serious crime. And make no mistake. We will hammer you if you don't tell the truth. We expect you to answer our questions not only truthfully, but as completely as possible. Don't leave out any details. We might ask a general question, but if we do, you need to respond with everything you know that might relate to that question. Absolutely everything. Don't wait for us to ask follow-ups."

Hardin leaned across the table and fixed his piercing ice-blue eyes on Frances.

Why is he looking at me like that? Frances thought, tapping his fingers on his legs. He looked around the room and back at Hardin, who was still staring at him.

Hardin raised his voice ever so slightly. "And by the way, we already know the answers to most of the questions we're going to ask you. We have talked to many people—many people both inside and outside the company—so we know what happened here. And we know that Otis was using inside information on some pretty big trades. So you're not going to fool us if you try to feed us a load of BS. You're just going to be digging your own grave."

Hardin inched back a bit, settled into his chair, and reverted to a calmer tone. He went over the agreement Frances already signed and all the ways it allowed the government to use Frances's statements against him if he lied during the meeting. The details were a blur, and Frances had a hard time listening to much of the speech.

His heart was pounding. *What can they possibly think I know that will help them? What can I say to keep them off my back? They're not going to believe the truth about how we make trading decisions.*

After Hardin finished his fire-and-brimstone monologue, Lois Lane, a.k.a. Annie Waters, took the baton. Waters had a calm, soothing voice and friendly tone. She even smiled once in a while. This seemed more like just a normal conversation. Frances thought he could talk to her. He relaxed his shoulders and leaned forward a little, trying to find a comfortable position in the rickety old chair. They covered basic background about Frances and his trading job at Otis.

"How does Otis make trading decisions? Can you describe the process?" Lois asked.

"Well, analysts in each group do research and write up recommendations on stocks they're covering," Frances explained.

"What kind of research do they do?" Lois inquired.

"As far as I know, they review public financial data and company filings, and also we have subscriptions to analyst reports from big financial institutions and such," Frances said. No one was writing any of this down. *They must already know all of this. Why go over it with me?* he wondered.

"Is there any policy or procedure to document these recommendations?"

Frances breathed easier and went into one of his prepared spiels. "Absolutely. The analysts write memos that are shared in this database we call the matrix. It's accessible to the top executives, the portfolio managers, the traders, and also legal and compliance. The memos are supposed to mention all the sources of information used for the trading recommendations so legal and compliance have a record."

"What about consultants? Does Otis use them too?"

Uh oh, here it comes, Frances thought.

He said, "Yeah, sure. All hedge funds use them, I think. Experts on different industries."

"These consultants—how did Otis vet those?" Annie asked. "What sort of diligence was done? You do know that a lot of these so-called 'expert' firms are just insider info-mills. Don't you? We've just sent a few of those guys to prison for five years."

"The truth is, I don't know too much about that, quite honestly. I'm just a trader. I don't know how the analysts choose the experts they hire; I don't even know which companies they use to find the experts."

"Really?" Hardin, who had been glancing at his phone during most of Frances's exchange with Annie, suddenly interjected. He stretched the syllables out as he said it—*reeeaallyy*—and rolled his eyes. "You've been working there for five years in an office of, what, twenty people? And you have no idea where the analysts find experts? Never heard any water cooler shop talk? Never had a beer with any of the analysts or portfolio managers where they told you about any juicy tips?"

One of the few fluorescent light bulbs that worked started to flicker.

Frances's pulse rate went up again, beating to the rhythm of the flickering light. "Um, I mean, sure, I'm friendly with those guys. Some of us hang out after work and go bar-hopping and stuff like that. But it's not like they talk to me about their sources. And—"

Frances looked over at Marc and then remembered one of the "talking points" Marc had given him during prep. "I mean, I do know that legal and compliance have to sign off on experts before we're allowed to use them. So I'm assuming…"

Hardin leaned over the table and gave Frances another one of those steely looks—the ones that made Frances feel like Hardin could see right through him. "Listen, Mr. O'Brien, we don't care what you *assume*. We want to know what you *know*. And as I said, I think we already know a lot of what you know. And frankly, I'm getting a very, very strong feeling that you are not telling us everything you know. And that—that is a big problem for you." Then Hardin shifted gears. "You play poker. Right? And you're actually a pretty good poker player. Aren't you?"

"Uh, yeah, I do." *Where's he going with this?* Frances thought. His palms suddenly felt clammy, and he rubbed his hands together. "As far as I know, that's not a federal crime. I go to Vegas. Gambling is legal there." He tapped his fingers on the table and shifted around in the chair again.

Hardin went in for the kill. "No, playing poker's not a crime, and betting is not a crime in Vegas. But you do know, don't you, that you have to pay taxes when you win. Right?"

"What do you mean? I—" Frances stammered.

Hardin glared at him. "Let me cut to the chase. We *know* all about your little tax evasion scam. We have your gambling records, and we know you didn't declare hundreds of thousands of winnings on your tax returns. And by the way, under the tax guidelines, you could be facing some serious jail time—"

"Hold on, hold on," interjected Marc Levy, Frances's attorney. "We need to take a time out. Can we have the room please?"

The prosecutors and Agent Marsh sauntered out and closed the door.

"Frances, what is this all about? Why didn't you tell me about this?"

Frances looked down dejectedly. "I guess I should have told you about this, but I never dreamed these guys would look at my tax returns. I thought they were only interested in securities stuff."

Marc gave him a withering look. "Listen, I told you I didn't want to hear anything for the first time in front of these guys. Let me talk to them. If they're serious about this tax thing, we may have to stop the interview. But I have a hunch the real issue is something about Otis that you're holding back."

"But what can it be?" *This is really going south*, Frances thought. His own lawyer was doubting him. Whose side was Marc on? "They're constantly training us on compliance. And people have been *especially* careful since a couple of years ago when Weisman brought down Paris Capital. So I really don't think anyone has a mole, and anyway if they do, they're not telling *me*. You've got to talk to them and figure out how to get me out of this."

"Look, I think it's too risky to continue this meeting until I have some more information—from you and from the prosecutors. We need to hit the pause button for now. I think that's gotta be it for today." Marc patted Frances on the back. "Don't worry. We'll figure this out. I've got a great relationship with Ted." He stepped out of the room, leaving Frances by himself.

Frances sat there for five, then ten, then fifteen minutes, waiting and tapping his wet Bruno Magli shoe repeatedly. His mind was racing. What were they talking about with Marc? Did they really care about gambling? Who actually paid taxes for that, anyway? Would they really send him to jail for not reporting his poker winnings? Would he lose his job if Otis found out about the gambling and tax evasion? What was he going to do if his mom found out about this?

His thoughts were suddenly interrupted by the flickering fluorescent light bulb, which made a *tzzt* noise and blew out.

Marc reentered the room. "C'mon, let's go. I think you're going to get another chance, but we'll need to do some more prep and come back again later."

Frances headed out to the hallway, where it was just a little bit brighter, and toward the elevator.

CHAPTER 3

THE INVESTIGATION (OBSTRUCTION PHASE)

APRIL 10, 2013

ONE SAINT ANDREW'S PLAZA, NEW YORK, NEW YORK

The pinkish-purple sky started to turn blue as Ted walked back to the office from the gym on Murray Street. The air was fresh and crisp but a little nippy—as if warning that winter was not yet over and one of those April snowstorms might still be coming. "We are the Champions" was playing in his earbuds. He felt pumped after adding ten pounds to his bench press routine and achieving a new personal best. The pace of the investigation was picking up, and it was going to be decision time soon. Might as well head back to the office and keep working on the case since he didn't have any other plans tonight. Ted felt his stomach rumble and grabbed some chicken takeout on the way.

He was back at his desk by the time the "blue hour" transformed into full-on night. He switched the music to his "thinking" playlist. As *Beethoven's Fifth Symphony* blasted into his ears, Ted poured over Otis emails from the week of March 12, 2012, and FBI reports of interviews of analysts from Otis's New York office. Interesting stuff, but how to make something of it?

Fingers tapping his desk, he pushed his chair back. It wasn't that late; Annie could still be around. He headed down the hall to her office. The door was ajar, and the light was on.

Ted knocked loudly and poked his head inside without waiting for her to answer. Her brown curls flicked back as she looked up at him from the pile of paper she was buried in. She smiled and said, "You're here late."

"Yeah, I was at the gym, and I decided, might as well come back here and do some more work," Ted replied.

"How was your workout?" Annie asked. "'I'm jealous. I skipped my run this morning to sleep an extra forty-five minutes."

It didn't make any difference, though, did it? Annie was one of those people who always looked fit and seemed like she never gained any weight, regardless of what she ate or whether she exercised. *Not like those of us who have to work to look good*, thought Ted. But then again, at least the work paid off.

He flexed his biceps, grinning. "It was good—fewer reps but more weight."

Ted looked over at the photo on the bookcase—a slightly younger version of Annie standing next to a smiling Chief Justice Roberts in his wood-paneled chambers. Everything seemed so easy for Annie. President of the *Harvard Law Review*, she was probably destined to be a famous Supreme Court lawyer or an appellate judge someday. Just like Ted's father, a prominent lawyer, giant of the New York bar, who clerked for Justice Brennan.

Ted was a decent student at NYU but didn't make law review. He had a great clerkship in the Southern District, though. His judge was a former US Attorney and had encouraged him to become a federal prosecutor. And it turned out Ted was a natural trial lawyer, even if he wasn't going to be the next Antonin Scalia or Ruth Bader Ginsburg—or his dad, or Annie. Maybe this case could be his big break—his chance to make a name for himself.

Ted grabbed one of the chairs in front of her desk and spun it backward. He sat down, leaned into its low back, and gazed at her intently. "Listen, I've been thinking. Maybe there's an obstruction case to be made. We serve a grand jury subpoena to Otis's expert quote-unquote consultant in early March. Then we follow up with one to Otis on March twelfth last year. It's broad. We are focused mostly on Delphun, but we want to cover the waterfront, just in case. So we ask Otis for documents relating to a bunch of funds and numerous trades."

Annie was listening, he thought, as his voice got more animated.

"And we know that Richard Ginsberg, who's now up in Boston, is tight with our friend Emma Simpson and her buddies in New York. Then boom, March fourteenth comes. It's just two days after the subpoena. Suddenly these guys in New York are telling everyone to destroy their notes with any evidence about where they got information used to make trading decisions. And all this stuff is shredded and deleted. Fishy as hell."

Annie motioned toward a stack of cases she was reading. "I've been looking into that. Remember the *Arthur Andersen* case—the one about the auditors destroying all those documents when the Enron scandal broke? Well, the Supreme Court was very specific. You need to prove corrupt intent." She paused.

"We need evidence that Simpson—and maybe Noguchi, too, since he's the one who sent the first email—*knew* about the subpoena. And we've got to find proof they knew the documents they were asking people to destroy were called for by the subpoena. I think that's the only way we make a case here."

"I hear you." Ted nodded. "But we do know documents were actually destroyed after Simpson's email. It's not clear whether they knew about the subpoena to Otis or the one to the consultant, sure. Still, a couple of employees had hard copy files of notes with consultants and stuff like that, which they tossed almost immediately after they got that email. It sounds like there was quite a frenzy of file-cleaning, in fact." His indigo eyes lit up like flashlights. "So they must have had something to hide, even if no one will fess up to what was incriminating about the trashed documents."

Ted leaned forward and rested his hands on the edge of Annie's desk. He really needed Annie to back his plan.

He said, "Here's what I'm thinking. Let's have the forensic guy look at the backup tapes to see if any electronic records were purged and can be recovered. If we find damning evidence was destroyed, that would be huge. We need to keep digging. I just know there's a coverup here."

Annie picked up her pen and began tapping it on her notepad. She sucked her lips into her mouth. Then she nodded and said, "It sure looks suspicious, and that's a good thought as to the backup tapes. But we've got to figure out what Simpson knew about the subpoena to Otis. It would be nice if we had some email to her about it. But I didn't see any evidence of anything like that in the emails sent after the subpoena was served."

She paused and twirled the pen in the air.

"Anyway, these analysts did throw stuff out. But like you said, I really don't think they knew the government had asked for their documents. So…"

Why did she always throw cold water on all Ted's ideas? He frowned.

Annie looked at him and then put the pen down, leaned forward, and said, "Wait a minute, what about that guy O'Brien? He must have gotten this email since it went to the whole New York office. Maybe he knows something or can give us some leads."

Ted's jaw tightened at first. How could he have forgotten about O'Brien? But then he relaxed a bit. What difference did that make? The good news was Annie wasn't giving up on the case yet. He needed her on board. "That's a great idea. I'll give Marc a call tomorrow. If O'Brien knows anything about this, we shouldn't have any problem getting it out of him. Not after that lousy meeting we had a few months ago."

He grinned and stood up, pleased with the plan. He glanced at his watch. "It's getting late. I think I'm going to head home in a few. How about you? Wanna grab a beer on the way home?"

Annie paused a minute, as if caught off guard. She seemed tempted, but then she shook her head. "No, thanks. Maybe some other time. I've got to do some work on another case, believe it or not. See you tomorrow."

A few minutes later, Ted headed back out into the night. The cool wind felt good, and he decided to walk home, which was just across the Brooklyn Bridge. New York could be a great city.

* * *

APRIL 30, 2013

ONE SAINT ANDREW'S PLAZA, NEW YORK, NEW YORK

Frances found himself heading toward the white tent in front of the prosecutors' office again. It was partly cloudy but a crisp spring day. He paced back and forth outside the entrance, waiting for Marc Levy. Biting his fingernails, Frances played their meeting last week over in his head. He thought about his daughter and the Dalton tuition bill sitting on his desk at home. How was he going to pay for it if he was in jail? And what about the mortgage? It was all well and good for Marc to blow this situation off as no big deal and tout his friendship with Hardin. But he wasn't the one whose life was being turned upside down.

In fact, the more he thought about it, this whole idea of meeting again with Superman and Lois Lane was a bad idea.

They couldn't just be interested in some random emails from a year ago. How was that any kind of crime? It didn't make sense. They must be trying to get at him. Was it too late to back out? Or would that put an even bigger target on his back? What had he done, anyway?

Frances was jolted out of his rumination by a tap on the back of his shoulder. Startled, he turned around to find Marc. "You okay? Ready?" Marc smiled and motioned toward the white tent. Frances's shoulders dropped as he stuck his hands in his pockets. He said nothing. They went inside and announced themselves to the expressionless guard.

Ten minutes later, they were back in the dingy conference room with Superman, Lois Lane, and baby-faced Agent Marsh. Someone had replaced the broken bulbs, but the room still had a dull tungsten glow that felt like a prison meeting room.

"Thanks for coming back, Mr. O'Brien. We hope you've had a chance to meet with your lawyer and think about where we left off last time. We *know* you have a lot of information that could be helpful to our investigation, so hopefully we can do a reset today." Lois had a businesslike tone. Her face was relaxed and not overtly hostile. "How long have you known Emma Simpson?" she asked.

"Emma?" He frowned. Where was this going? "I've known her since I joined Otis about five years ago."

"So you worked with her then?" Lois stopped twirling her pen in the air. When he nodded, she asked, "What was she like to work with?"

"Back then she was a portfolio manager. She was a good colleague. Friendly and supportive."

Lois put her pen down and leaned forward slightly. "Were you surprised when she became head of the New York office?"

That's kind of a weird question, isn't it? Frances thought as he bit his lips. "Um, not really. Her fund was always one of the top performers."

"Why was she picked over Marshall Minnow? Wasn't he more senior?" Lois asked pointedly.

"That's true, but you know, those decisions are way above my pay grade," said Frances. "What I do know is that her funds made a lot more money. She was a little more willing to take on risk; he's more old-school and conservative in his approach to his sector."

Lois nodded and gave Superman a knowing look.

What was that about? Frances wondered. *Maybe I shouldn't have said that.* Perhaps office politics are a safer topic. "And she seemed to get along really well with the top brass—especially our current CEO, Richard Ginsberg, who was then running the New York operation."

"Richard Ginsberg—isn't he working in Boston now?" Lois asked casually. "How'd that come about?"

Frances breathed a little easier. She didn't seem too interested in him, did she? He was more comfortable answering questions about other people, even if he couldn't figure out where they were going.

He said, "Well, I'm not too sure. But Boston's funds weren't doing that great, and our CEO at the time was looking to make a change to try and shake things up there. I think Richard had some personal reason to move—family up there or something—so he jumped at the opportunity. That was when Emma got promoted." Frances brushed back a thick wave of his auburn hair. "I don't really work directly with her that much anymore. She still manages one of her old funds, but she mostly works with another trader on that."

Wait, Frances thought. *Why isn't Agent Marsh taking any notes? What do they expect me to say?* He sat back a bit and crossed his arms.

"Well, we'll get to that, but let's talk about the days before she ran the office. Didn't you work with her then? Weren't you one of her main traders?" Lois was in rapid-fire mode suddenly. Still calm, but her brow was furrowed. Her hazel eyes transformed from yellowish-green to a darker, almost chocolate hue.

"Sure. Emma was fine to work with. She had really good instincts about the markets. She was pretty no nonsense and didn't have time for chitchat or a lot of patience. I mean, I don't know her that well. She doesn't hang out after work or go out with the traders or anything. She commutes upstate and she's got two kids, so she's always running out early, and she often works from home on Fridays."

Agent Marsh still hadn't picked up his pen. Out of the corner of his eye, Frances saw Superman with his elbows on the table. He was slowly rubbing his hands together—back and forth, back and forth, back and forth. He glared right at Frances, unblinking. Frances felt a pit in his stomach. He leaned forward slightly, as if readying himself to block a gut-punch.

Then Superman abruptly stopped his hand motions, weaved his fingers together, and leaned forward. "Dude, we didn't haul you in here to talk about Ms. Simpson's work-life balance routine. We don't have all day. Tell us about her fund. How did she do so well? Did she have any quote-unquote consultants? What was her secret sauce?"

Frances's fingers, now clammy with beads of sweat, found their way through that Jimmy Neutron-like wave in his hair again. "In all honesty, like I said before, I really don't know much about where the analysts and the portfolio managers get information. I think all of them used consultants, and they were supposed to get the consultants approved by compliance."

Superman raised himself up slightly from his seat as his elbows pushed down on the chair's arms. He was about to pounce again. *He thinks she cheats and that I'm covering for her*, Frances thought.

He quickly shifted gears. "Now, *could* she have been cutting corners? Is it possible she had moles or sources she talked to on the inside? Of course it's possible. But she wouldn't have told me. I'm being totally honest here. I really don't know." Frances's voice shook as he looked straight into Ted Hardin's steely eyes, begging for assurance.

Hardin leaned back, his large frame filling the decaying black leather armchair. "Okay, so *if* Emma Simpson had any dirty sources, who would know? Who was she tight with; who did she confide in?"

Frances realized he was tugging on his hair, so he stopped. "She's pretty close to Ben Noguchi. He's one of the top portfolio managers and helps her run the New York office. Also Richard, who's now in Boston, like I mentioned earlier."

That seemed to satisfy Hardin, at least for now. Hardin nodded to Annie Waters, who opened a binder, perused a document, and looked up at Frances inquisitively. "So, let's switch gears a bit. Do you remember how you first learned about our investigation?"

Finally, Frances thought, *sounds like the territory we went over last week in Marc's office*. "Yes, it was last March. The portfolio managers have these weekly meetings with the top analysts for each fund. Emma Simpson, Doug Jones—he's from legal and compliance—and usually Ben. I don't go to them. The traders aren't invited. But afterward I remember someone telling me they heard Doug say at the meeting that there was an investigation. There was some chatter about that; people were wondering what was going on."

"At that time, did you learn anything more specific? Did you know it was a criminal investigation? Any rumors or scuttlebutt about what was being investigated?" Lois asked.

"Not really," replied Frances. "Something about a subpoena. That's about it."

"When in March was this? Do you remember?" Lois asked nonchalantly.

"I'm not too sure," said Frances. "I mean, it was last year. I don't really remember."

Lois leaned forward and looked straight at him. "Well, can you try to give us your best estimate? I mean, did anything happen in March to help pinpoint the date—a birthday, some personal event, or something that happened around the same time?"

Frances paused and racked his brains. "Okay—maybe sometime around St. Paddy's Day? It's possible I heard it when a few of us went out to drink green beer that night after work. That's my best guess. But I have no idea what day it actually happened."

The two prosecutors exchanged a knowing look.

Lois asked, "And these weekly meetings with the portfolio managers, do you know if they're held on a particular day of the week?"

"Wednesdays, I think," Frances responded. Agent Marsh seemed distracted, but Ted touched his shoulder and pointed at his pen. Marsh began jotting down some notes.

"Now, are you familiar with Otis's so-called document retention policy?" Lois asked.

Frances heard a *thwack* as she pulled open the metal binder rings and then handed him a sheet of paper with an email on it.

"Did you receive this email? It was dated Wednesday, March 14, 2012."

Frances took a quick look and confirmed it was the same document Marc had shown him in prep. "Yes, this is an email Ben sent to everyone in the office. The policy he's referring to explains how long we're supposed to keep different records and when we're not supposed to keep documents."

He looked at Waters, who appeared to be listening carefully. "For instance, I think I may have mentioned this last time, there's this database—matrix, it's called—where all the backup for trades is supposed to be kept. It has analyst reports and stuff like that. But if anyone has handwritten research notes, they're not supposed to keep those once they complete a memo or analyst report—only the final typed report goes into the matrix."

"So," Hardin interjected, "what was your reaction to this email? Did it seem odd? Did it come out of the blue, or were emails like this common?"

"Well, I wouldn't say this was common, but it didn't seem *odd*. I didn't think too much about it at the time, especially since he was in charge of the computer upgrade and the email talks about that too. But anyway, I don't really take many notes in my job—not anything I would keep. Our trades are recorded in the computer system, just like our emails and Bloomberg 'chats,' so there wasn't much for me to do in response. I think this was more directed at the analysts."

Waters took the baton back. "Well, do you know what, if anything, any analysts or anyone else did in response to this email? It went to everyone in New York, didn't it?" As Frances nodded, Waters took another piece of paper out of her binder and placed it in front of him. "And Emma Simpson resent it to everyone later that same day, didn't she?" Waters stared at Frances. "She was the boss, right? People pay attention when the boss sends instructions, don't they?"

Frances looked around the room nervously and then back at the email. The truth was, he didn't even remember the email until Marc showed it to him last week. But they seemed to think it was pretty nefarious.

"Um, well, I assume everyone read it, and so the people who had materials to throw out would have done that—especially since, I guess, the email was sent twice, first by Ben, and then again by Emma. And the reference to lawsuits and regulatory inquiries—I mean, that must have caught folks' attention. So I'm sure people started deleting their files and throwing out notes…"

As the words escaped his mouth, Frances heard himself throwing Emma under the bus. *Wait, what?* Did he really just say that? Had he sunk that low? But everyone seemed to be smiling.

Waters closed her black binder loudly. Hardin looked at his watch. "Listen, we have another meeting in a few minutes, so we need to wrap this up, but we'll probably need to speak with you again. Thanks for coming in today. This was very helpful," he said.

Then they left.

Frances let out a sigh of relief. He stood up, unstuck his pants from his clammy legs, and followed them out.

CHAPTER 4

LAWYERING UP

—

JULY 3, 2013

885 THIRD AVENUE, NEW YORK, NEW YORK

The subway car was half empty when Emma boarded the northbound M train at Bryant Park, but she still made sure to find a seat at the end of a row and away from other passengers. At least it was air conditioned today. Thankfully she was not walking the fifteen blocks to this meeting with her new lawyer in the sweltering heat. She clutched the blue suit jacket on her lap. The only other time she'd needed a personal lawyer was when they bought the farm. But that was just a real estate guy. The meeting this afternoon was with a *criminal* lawyer—someone who specialized in white collar defense.

Did she really need a lawyer? It was obviously a big problem that Peter Weisman, Mr. Media Darling US Attorney, seemed to have his sights on Otis Capital and another big headline about taking down a hedge fund. But until last week, this wasn't Emma's *personal* problem. It was a minor distraction, something the Boston office and their media group were supposed to be dealing with. And Richard had assured her there was nothing there. Her group didn't even invest in the media sector anymore. And no one ever told her Weisman was investigating any funds under her purview.

Not until last week, that is.

At the time, Emma had just learned one of her pet projects—a drug company everyone warned her to avoid like the plague—was about to be purchased by a "Big Pharma" company.

Ben came running into her office. "I can't believe it!" he said. "Where'd you get that crystal ball? I thought for sure things were over when they had to pause the clinical trial for that immunotherapy drug. Who knew it would get approved by the FDA two years later?"

"I learned everything there was to know about that drug." Her voice trailed off as she glanced at her bookshelf and saw her dad, with then-little Sarah in his lap, gazing back and smiling at her. As if to say, *I'm still here watching over you. Don't worry.* "You know, it was personal for me. We'd tried everything else. I never talked about it, but my dad got into the trial. It was the only thing that could have saved his life." She paused. "And it did, for about six months. But the reality was, his diagnosis came too late for any miracle cures. I guess he would've been pleased to know that he helped them test an effective treatment so others could survive the disease."

She reflected back on how, even his final days, despite the tremendous pain, he never lost his sense of humor or grace.

The bittersweet moment, however, was interrupted a few minutes later. Doug barged in, ignoring the hushed tones of her conversation with Ben. "Listen, guys, Weisman has shifted gears. Now he's targeting our New York operation—including you two."

He explained that documents were destroyed while Otis was responding to the subpoena. Apparently some emails about the document retention policy—which Emma barely remembered—created a huge problem. So now Emma and several New York colleagues were being told to lawyer up.

Emma tugged at her pearls. She didn't understand why the company's lawyers couldn't handle this. Did she really need her own big-shot defense lawyer? The company already had a very expensive law firm with a bunch of former federal prosecutors handling the subpoena. Was there something they weren't telling her?

At least they recommended a few good people, including the one she'd chosen, Will Shelby. He had impressive credentials. Three degrees from Yale, a federal clerkship, a tour at a top DC firm, experience as a federal public defender. And a great track record on the defense side.

The subway car lurched to a stop at 53rd Street, shaking Emma back to reality. She sped to the escalator to Third Avenue, which seemed like it would never end. Emma felt like she was emerging from the bowels of a dark, steamy cauldron, and the way out at the top kept getting further away. So she started walking up the escalator and passing people just standing there until she finally got to the street.

There it was. The "Lipstick" building—a pinkish, modern oval skyscraper designed by famed architect Philip Johnson. It looked more like a pencil-shaped three-layer cake than lipstick, actually. Emma put on her jacket as she entered the building. She presented her ID to the guard, who sent her up to reception on the thirtieth floor—the top tier of the cake.

A tall, elegant man in a midnight blue designer suit greeted her there with a warm smile and an outstretched hand. He looked just like Idris Elba. "I'm Will Shelby. It's really nice to meet you," he said.

Emma smiled. "I would say the same, but…"

"I know. I know." Shelby laughed. "In my line of work, it's rare that anyone is happy to have a need for my services. But don't worry. I won't take it personally."

He led her into a conference room bathed in sunlight, where he introduced a baby-faced associate named Josh.

"You want anything to drink?" He motioned toward a credenza with several neat rows of Fiji water bottles and a carafe of coffee next to gleaming white mugs emblazoned "SAB."

Emma grabbed a water bottle and took a seat facing the East River and Queens.

Shelby sat down across from her. "Listen, I know you're not happy to be here. It's an unfortunate situation."

"To be honest, I don't really know too much about why I'm here," Emma said. "I thought this was an investigation about a stock one of our media and entertainment sector funds invested in. As I told you on our call, our Boston office runs those funds. I don't manage those portfolios or supervise the people who do."

Will nodded. "I know. I know. And it's true that this may have started because of some Delphun trades that worked out very well for that media fund. But according to Otis's lawyers, the subpoena to Otis was very broad and sought all kinds of records over a multiyear period—about trades in *all* the funds. And—"

Emma's eyes widened and her lips tightened. *What?* "This is the first I'm hearing about that."

"I'm not surprised." Shelby said as he shook his head. "Look, that's a good thing, believe it or not."

He took a long sip of his coffee.

"The key to this, I think, is what you knew—or rather, didn't know—back in March 2012. Frankly, you'd be in a heap of trouble if you had known about the subpoena to Otis and how broad it was when you sent that email."

Shelby's voice was deep and mellifluous. He looked at Emma intently.

"But there's no case without that. So let's go through the facts today. Josh and I need to know everything—your background, your job duties, everything you remember about the events relating to the email."

"Sounds good," said Emma, "though frankly I barely remember these events."

"Don't worry. We can help refresh your recollection," Shelby said as Josh placed a binder of documents in front of Emma.

She opened the water bottle and placed her jacket on the back of the chair. Then Emma looked at the two of them, and her eyes lit up a brilliant blue. "Okay, fire away."

"Why don't you start by telling us a bit about your personal background and then how you got to Otis and what roles you've had there."

"Well, I grew up mostly here in the city. My parents were professors, and when I was about twelve, we moved to Paris for a few years so they could teach at a French university, but then we returned and I finished high school here."

That had been a rough adjustment at first, but Emma left those details out.

"I started working at Otis about eleven years ago after I left Goldman Sachs. Otis was fairly new at the time, so it was an opportunity to get in on the ground floor. They told me after a year I'd get to manage my own portfolio, so I'd be making decisions about what to invest in for certain funds rather than just gathering data and making recommendations. But that didn't actually happen until about three years after I started."

In fact, she'd been passed over in favor of Marshall for one position, but she didn't mention that either.

"Eventually, they gave me a media fund to manage, and it did really well, so when we decided to start some health care funds, our CEO asked me to run them. I did that for about five years before they asked me to head the New York office," Emma said.

The conversation continued for a couple of hours. Emma took the lawyers through Otis's procedures, her role as head of the New York office, and the events of March 14, 2012.

Then Emma headed back outside, bracing for that feeling of stepping into a sauna. But it didn't come. The air was still heavy, but what hit her was a tuft of lukewarm air. No point in returning to the oppressive underground heat of the subway. Instead, Emma put on her sunglasses and started walking back to her office.

It was good to get some exercise.

* * *

JULY 4, 2013

PITCHER LANE, RED HOOK, NEW YORK

Glimmers of soft golden light peeked through the haze to illuminate a few chunks of grass on the front lawn. They created a patchwork of yellowish green interspersed with darker green dots formed by the shade of the gathering clouds. Pierre Elis gazed out at the tranquil scene, pondering various grape varietals. Then the calm scene was suddenly disrupted by a group of wild turkeys scurrying across the front yard.

A few years ago, Pierre's first thought upon seeing these turkeys was curiosity and wonder at the beauty of nature. He would make sure the children saw them, delight in watching them chase the turkeys around the lawn, and perhaps try to grab a few photos if he could.

But now, the children were older and unlikely to be interested. What was top of mind was that these were pests—enemies that could destroy his dream. Just like those cottontail rabbits popping up all over the neighborhood that used to seem so cute. Would the fencing around the newly planted grape vines keep them away from his precious crops?

Pierre was sitting at the desk he'd made himself—a large, polished slab of cherry wood—in his home office doing some research for the winery he was building. The office was in a perfect corner of the house. It had huge windows and was filled with light on sunny days. The desk faced south, with a view of the front lawn and the vineyard across the road from the house.

It's too bad it takes so long for my grapes to be ready, he thought. *The sooner we can market wines from grapes grown here, the sooner I can start to turn a profit. Then maybe Emma will appreciate why we poured so much money into this project.*

Just then Ghost and Dyer started barking up a storm.

Pierre looked up from his computer. *Colin must be here.* Sure enough, a black Volvo station wagon was pulling into the driveway. Pierre's buddy, Colin Barr, was spending the July 4th holiday in Dutchess County with his family and was stopping by for a visit this afternoon. Pierre looked forward to showing him the winery.

Pierre and Colin met in the 1990s when they were summer associates at a law firm in Washington, DC. They had been good friends ever since. They'd married and moved to New York around the same time, and their children were similar ages. Their career paths diverged quickly after that fateful summer, however. Colin ended up clerking on the Second Circuit and doing a stint as a prosecutor. He eventually landed a partnership at a big law firm, where he was now head of the appellate practice group.

Pierre initially practiced corporate law for a brief period, but his true passion was haute cuisine and wine. So after a few years he jumped at an offer to work in-house at the Jean-Georges Restaurant Group, hoping eventually to transition to the business side. That never happened, because he and Emma moved to the country instead. But he had no regrets. This was a much better environment for the kids to grow up in. Besides, he liked the challenge of starting his own business.

Pierre strode to the front door and went outside. The dogs were quieter now, but they surrounded Colin with their tails wagging frantically as he petted them.

"Bonjour, Colin, it's so great to see you!" Pierre flashed a big smile as he broke through the dog wall and gave his friend a bear hug.

Colin grinned and said, "It's been way too long, buddy."

Pierre ushered him into the kitchen. "How've you been?" The two chatted for a while, catching up on the latest gossip about mutual friends and bragging about the recent exploits of their children. Then Pierre said, "C'mon let me give you the grand tour. Let's go before the thunderstorms start. I want to show you what I did with that old barn."

They walked out into the sunshine. Pierre led the way down the road toward the red barn he had renovated and outfitted with winemaking equipment.

They passed the fields with the neat rows of grape vines. "These are the grapes we've planted so far," Pierre said. "It will take about three years before we can actually harvest them and start making wine, but I'm buying grapes while we're waiting so I can start experimenting with the process."

"What kind of wine?" asked Colin.

"Chardonnay and pinot noir to start with. That's what I've planted, so I figure it makes sense to buy the same type of grape for the transition phase," Pierre explained. "These vines came from Napa and Sonoma, but I'm thinking about planting some other ones from newer domestic regions, like Long Island and Virginia."

They walked over to the barn, where Pierre inhaled the fresh wooded smell of the newly installed oak barrels. He showed off the crush pad equipment, fermenters, filtration system, and bottling gear and explained how the wine would be manufactured.

"It's closed today, but we're already using the tasting room to serve people who tour the first wine we've made—a light pinot. Want to try it? I might have some La Tur cheese and crackers here too."

"Sure, why not? Just one glass, though. It's early," said Colin.

They sat at the new picnic table Pierre had just installed under the big Japanese maple near the barn door. Pierre loved that tree—the intricately shaped leaves and their brilliant red color. And it cast a serene, zen-like shade that provided a touch of relief on this hot, hazy day.

This would be a perfect time to ask for Colin's counsel about Emma's dilemma. Pierre could use a bit of advice about the potential risks and charges that could be brought. He had no idea if her lawyer, Will Shelby, was any good, and Colin probably knew the guy. He was always a good judge of these types of things.

Pierre tapped his foot on the ground and twisted the corkscrew slowly until the cork popped out. He frowned. On the other hand, it was probably best to keep this under wraps. Emma would be furious if she found out he was telling people about the investigation. And based on her report after meeting with Shelby, there was probably nothing to worry about anyway.

Pierre said instead, "So how's your work? Any interesting new cases?"

"As a matter of fact, I just won a big appeal because of juror misconduct." Colin's eyes lit up.

Uh oh, he has that look, thought Pierre. *Maybe I shouldn't have asked. This could take a while.*

It did. Colin launched into his current favorite subject. "This juror lied through her teeth to get on the jury, if you can believe that. She was a suspended lawyer but pretended to be a housewife who only had a college degree. Plus, she said her husband was a bus driver, but it turned out he was a convicted mobster. Lied about her address to make herself more 'marketable' as a juror. And that's just part of it," Colin said.

"Get this," he continued. "After the trial—which lasted several months—she wrote a letter to one of the prosecutors, talking about what a great job he did and saying a bunch of things showing she was biased against the defendants from the get-go. Long story short, the trial judge held a hearing, found she was biased, and granted a new trial for some of the defendants, but not my client. He said my client's trial lawyers should have known who the juror really was because they googled the names during jury selection. He tried to blame them for the fiasco."

"Sounds like he got a raw deal," Pierre said. "It seems so odd the judge would grant a new trial for some but not all. Also, that woman sounds like a real kook. Why would anyone want to serve on a jury for a long trial?" Colin's job sure sounded more fun than the late hours of due diligence on corporate deals Pierre did as an associate. "So, what happened? You got the verdict overturned on appeal?" he asked.

There was a loud thunderclap. Pierre looked up. Several large gray clouds had covered up the sun.

"Yes," Colin bragged. "And then I persuaded the government to drop the case rather than retry it." Then he scrunched up his mouth in disgust. "And frankly, the case against my client was BS anyway. The charges related to these tax shelters, but my guy was just a broker who arranged some trades. He worked at a big financial institution, and their compliance department approved the transactions." Colin shook his head. "He had no idea the tax treatment was wrong."

Pierre felt a few raindrops. "That is awful. I don't understand why they would charge your guy. Sounds like he was just a minor witness to the whole thing."

Colin said, "Hard to say. Could be that he worked for a big bank, and the government was investigating other stuff at the bank, which ended up paying a big fine." Colin took a sip of wine. "But my poor guy was collateral damage—and he would have gone to prison if we'd lost the appeal." Then Colin's face turned flush as he got more animated. "The worst part is that by the time we won the appeal, my client had been living under a cloud for five years. He lost his job, his reputation was tarred, and his family suffered. It was just awful."

Pierre looked at his feet, suddenly feeling a chill from the gathering storm. "Maybe we should talk about something more pleasant." Then he quickly gathered the glasses and what was left of the cheese. "C'mon, let's go back to the house before we get soaked."

Better not tell Emma that story, Pierre thought as he flew down the road, leaving Colin in his wake, struggling to catch up. *Next time I'll ask Colin about his latest copyright appeal instead.*

CHAPTER 5

SLEEPING DOGS?

NOVEMBER 16, 2013

BEAR MOUNTAIN STATE PARK, NEW YORK

Thwwwack, thwwack, thwack went the pucks hitting the glass.
Pierre closed his eyes for a moment and just listened. This

was a form of meditation for him. He focused his brain on the sounds of the skaters whirring around the rink during the pregame drills. The rhythmic *tap, tap, tap* of the sticks' blades cradling the puck as skaters maneuvered around the cones. The familiar *ksssh-ksssh-ksssh*, as the skates whizzed around, cutting up the ice. The *ping!* of pucks hitting the metal rods of the net.

These soothing sounds brought back memories of Pierre's childhood exploits on the rink. Well, not actual exploits. More like fantasies about what those exploits could have been with a little more talent.

Fortunately, Pierre thought, *Sarah did not inherit my mediocre hockey skills.* She was a natural. She started skating when she was two years old and was zooming around rinks by the time she was about five. She was fearless. Before long, she was leaving some older and bigger children—boys and girls alike—in the dust. Her brother, Daniel, saw the writing on the wall when it became apparent that his seven-year-old sister was the faster skater. On his ninth birthday, he asked for an official NFL football and announced that he hated hockey: "I only do sports played in sneakers with real balls, and that's that!"

As the sounds ebbed, Pierre opened his eyes. The skaters were bunched up in their huddle with the coach before the opening whistle. The first glimmers of sun were starting to emerge on the horizon as the sky was transforming from dark navy to pinkish-purplish tones. *Is it really worth waking up at the crack of dawn for these early morning games?* he thought, glancing at the scoreboard clock just as it flashed 7:00 a.m. He felt a chill on his neck and pulled up the hood of his parka. He grinned and shouted, "Go, Fillies!" as the skaters lined up for the opening face-off.

Sarah won the face-off, but a couple of passes and a missed shot later, the other team had seized the advantage and taken the action back to the Fillies' defensive zone. "C'mon, take it back, take it back!" he yelled. "Dammit," he muttered as they seemed to have done so but the whistle blew for an offsides call. He felt a tap on the shoulder and turned around to find Emma handing him a steaming hot paper cup.

"Here you go, P," she said. "I got some donuts too."

"Now, why would you do that? Do you want me to die before I'm sixty?" he replied, half-smiling. "No thanks. I'll wait until after the game and get a proper breakfast with some protein."

Why did she always do this? She could eat as many donuts as she wanted and wouldn't gain an ounce. But they both knew he was not so lucky in the metabolism department. When his doctor once told him to lose five pounds, he complained about Emma's inability ever to gain weight. The doctor was neither sympathetic nor politically correct. He responded by asking Pierre: "Would you rather have a fat wife?" Which was a good point, he supposed.

"Sorry," Emma said sheepishly. "I just couldn't resist. This place has these amazing homemade cider donuts. The smell was irresistible. And they were still warm. I'll give the rest to the girls after the game. I promise." She turned her gaze to the ice. "Is this team good?"

"They've got some decent skaters, and I've heard they play tough defense—rough defense, in fact. But I don't think they have any great puck-handlers—" As if on cue, one of the opposing players lost control of the puck.

Sarah materialized out of nowhere. Her stick was a puck magnet, and she whooshed down the ice on a breakaway. Just as she started to aim a shot at the goal, a defender chasing her shoved a stick in front of her skate. Sarah tripped, the puck went flying past the goal, and the opposing team took it back to their offensive zone.

The referees did nothing.

"Putain, qu'est-ce que c'est?" Pierre yelled at the refs. "Where's the whistle?"

"That was blatant tripping! She could have smashed her head into the ice." Emma was freaking out. "I don't know why we let her play this sport. It's so dangerous! You'd think they'd at least enforce the rules to protect these kids."

"Oh, c'mon. When I played, they didn't even make us wear helmets!" Pierre said. "But those refs are a disgrace. They never call any penalties, even when we play these dirty teams. And the head ref is an FBI agent! You'd think she, of all people, would enforce the rules."

"Ugh, just what we need." Emma grimaced. "Feds asleep at the switch, focused on the wrong things." She looked away from the action into the distance, suddenly marooned in her own thoughts.

Pierre flinched. Why had he mentioned the FBI? That was stupid. They hadn't talked about the "issue" in months. He hadn't thought about in a while and, he assumed, neither had she. "Sorry, didn't mean to remind you—"

Emma took a deep breath and looked back at the ice. "It's okay," she said, suddenly tapping her hands on the rink's glass wall. "There's probably nothing to worry about. Will's presentation was two months ago. It's been radio silence ever since." She took her hands off the glass and cracked her knuckles. Then she scrunched up her mouth and took a deep breath. "No news is probably good news, right?"

"Yeah, I think so," Pierre said. "Has Will checked in with them recently?"

"No," Emma replied. "He said he'd rather not poke the bear. Maybe they're concerned with what he said, or maybe they're focused on other cases and will lose interest."

Pierre nodded. "Yeah, I guess it's best to let sleeping dogs lie. Let's not think about it."

Emma put her hands in her pockets. She had that glassy-eyed look again as her gaze drifted away to the mountains.

All of a sudden the Fillies' bench and their fans were on their feet and roaring again. Pierre grabbed Emma's hand and pointed to center ice. Sarah flashed by like lightning. Then the red light atop the opposing goal was flashing, and the Fillies were dancing around the ice with their sticks in the air, celebrating.

The crowd erupted in cheers of, "Goal, goal, goal," as the players assembled for the next face-off.

Emma went inside to get more coffee while Pierre debated whether to shoot the game. He would love to photograph Sarah in action. On the other hand, if he took out his camera, he'd obsess about documenting everything instead of just watching her play. Plus, it always seemed like a jinx. When he used it, the other team controlled the puck all the time. *Screw it, I'll just watch*, he thought.

He felt his pocket vibrate and pulled out his phone to see a text from Daniel. "Can you bring back a clam pizza from Pepe's?"

"No, dude, Yonkers isn't on the way home. It's fifty minutes *south* of here!"

"Are you sure? That pizza is sooooooo good," came the response.

"Yeah, I'm sure!"

Emma returned. She glanced at his phone. "What are we going to do about him?" She shook her head. "When is he going to grow up? He's fifteen years old."

"Oh, come on. Give him some time," Pierre said. "We all do stupid things when we're teenagers."

"But why would he do *that*? We've told him so many times to be careful with social media. Especially after Larsen got suspended last year for those awful posts about the girls' swim team."

"The kid was just letting off some steam." Pierre rolled his eyes. "Besides, it was kind of justified. Don't forget, we were pissed off too." Pierre felt himself getting flushed just reliving how Daniel got screwed during basketball tryouts. "How could they cut him from the varsity team? That coach is obsessed with height. Daniel's faster than anyone else; he's the best three-point shooter on the team. But the coach thought he was too short and that Daniel didn't kiss his ass enough."

"I know. I know. That was bullshit." Emma twisted her mouth. "But did he really have to go on Snapchat and send a message to 250 people? Telling the school, the basketball team, the coach, and the town, to 'fuck off'?" She snorted. "And now he can't even play on the JV team this year." She crossed her arms and turned toward the rink.

"But he shouldn't be punished at all for this. C'est ridicule." Pierre frowned. "Isn't there supposed to be free speech in America? It's not like he did it in the school either. Since when does the school get to police a student's private speech on the internet?"

"Maybe so, but he has no judgment." Emma pushed her palm into her forehead. "And what if colleges find out about it? How could he be so stupid?"

Pierre bit his lip and turned away. He felt a sudden chill and pulled his hood over his head and crossed his arms tightly.

Emma was so tough on Daniel. Of course, it was because she loved him and worried about him. But was that how Daniel saw it? Or did he just think she had impossible expectations?

He tried to turn his attention back to the game and rid his mind of the tension. Sarah was rotating off for a rest. He closed his eyes and breathed in and out. *Focus*, he told himself. *Listen to the soothing and familiar noises of the skates cutting the ice, the stick tapping the puck, the noises of the crowd around you.*

Just as he was breathing a little easier, the buzzer sounded.

He opened his eyes and glanced at the scoreboard. Apparently he missed two goals, but the Fillies won, two to one.

CHAPTER 6

THE CHARGING
DECISION

———

FEBRUARY 10, 2014

ONE SAINT ANDREW'S PLAZA, NEW YORK, NEW YORK

The ground was caked with a thin layer of white dust as Annie stepped out into the swirling flakes. She pulled up the hood of her red parka as the cold wind slapped her face. Days like this reminded her of home, but she wasn't as tough as she used to be. A decade on the East Coast would do that to you. Back in Saint Paul, fourteen-degree weather would not faze her—in fact, her only concern probably would be whether it would be too snowy to play pond hockey after school. Now she was grateful the walk to the subway was so short.

Annie left the wind and churning snow in her wake as she descended into the Central Park West 81st Street station. The train pulled up as she reached the platform.

Today was the day. After two and a half years investigating Otis, it was time to put up or shut up.

The team was meeting with the Chief of the Criminal Division and US Attorney Peter Weisman. The topic was whether to go forward with the obstruction case against Emma Simpson and Ben Noguchi or close the book on Otis. The meeting was originally scheduled the week before, as a "check-in" on case status. But things had heated up since then.

As the train rumbled downtown, Annie thumbed through her email, replaying the previous afternoon's events in her mind.

She and Ted were going over their latest interview with Lucy Malomar, Otis's assistant general counsel. As usual, Ted was viewing the testimony through a more incriminating lens than Annie was.

"Ted," she'd said, "Malomar didn't actually speak to Simpson about the investigation or the subpoena. She wasn't even in the meeting the day we think Simpson learned about it. Our case on her knowledge is razor-thin."

Ted, of course, was not buying her argument. "So what if *she* didn't speak to her? Her testimony about the retention policy and the subpoena itself is great, and she told Doug Jones about the investigation. And Jones is the New York compliance guy and was in the morning meeting the day Simpson sent the email."

Annie was dumbfounded. What was Ted thinking? Did he even care whether she was guilty or whether they could prove it? Or did he just want a big high-profile trial to stick on his résumé so he could make millions at a big Wall Street firm next year?

Then, before she could respond, Ted looked up from his phone and flashed a smug grin. "Apparently I'm not the *only* one who feels this way. Have a look at this email we just got from Jared—and *Peter*. It seems like this case has their attention, big time. And it's a chance for us to grab the headlines back from Eastern."

The US Attorney's Office in Manhattan—otherwise known as the "Sovereign District of New York"—was not known for humility or deference to others in the broader Department of Justice "team." They were especially dismissive of their friends across the river in Brooklyn's Eastern District of New York. They saw the world as it was depicted in the famous 1976 *New Yorker* cover: Manhattan was the center of the earth, and the rest of the United States and everything beyond the Pacific Ocean was diminutive by comparison.

Annie sighed and read the email chain. Great, now the bosses were throwing a match on Ted's jug of gasoline.

Peter had sent Jared a press release from the Eastern District announcing a takedown of the top foreign exchange traders at a big Wall Street bank. Eastern had arrested five of these guys on headline-grabbing market manipulation charges. Peter's loaded message of "????" hovered atop the press release. In other words, this was Peter's polite way of saying, "Where the fuck were *we* in this big case?"

This latest Eastern District case poured salt into a sore wound the Sovereign District was nursing. It was as if the twenty-seven-time world champion New York Yankees missed the playoffs but the Mets won the World Series. Yet the past year had been a slow one without many headline-grabbing cases. The Office's (and Weisman's) reputation as *the* cop of Wall Street seemed to be slipping away.

And what was Jared's response to Weisman's bitching about Eastern's hot new case? Predictably, to light a fire under Ted and Annie to relieve the pressure *Jared* was getting from Weisman. His message to Annie and Ted: "We need to MOVE the Otis case."

This was all Annie needed, right when she was trying to restrain Ted and *reason* with him, she thought as the train rumbled to a halt at Chambers Street. She disembarked and braced herself to face the storm.

* * *

A few minutes later, Annie was sitting with Ted and Jared in the eighth-floor conference room next to the US Attorney's personal office, waiting to see Peter and the Criminal Division Chief. She wrapped her hands, still icy from the trek downtown, around her porcelain mug to warm them as she took a few sips of coffee.

She glanced around the conference room with its wood paneling, its rows of US reports and federal reporters, its big shiny wooden table, and its American flag. It had no windows, but unlike the decrepit conference space down in the securities unit, this room was classy. Annie wasn't up here much, but every time she was, she thought back to her first visit to this room four years earlier, when she had taken her oath of office.

Annie's reflections were interrupted by Peter's assistant, who summoned the group into his cavernous office. The Criminal Division Chief, Philip "Mac" McCarthy, was already there. McCarthy was one of the most competitive people Annie had ever encountered, as she'd learned after agreeing to a tennis match with him last fall. What started as a friendly match between two former Harvard tennis team stars turned into a knock-down, drag-out fight. The match lasted an extra hour because every time Annie (who was, after all, ten years younger) got the edge, McCarthy would insist on another game. She should have known. He'd been an incredibly aggressive defense lawyer, the type who made your life hell with constant discovery motions, misconduct accusations, whatever it took. But now that he'd returned to the Office to lead the Criminal Division, he was the most zealous prosecutor imaginable.

Annie took a spot on the end of Weisman's large leather couch next to Jared. Ted sat on his other side. Weisman and McCarthy sat across from them in matching side chairs. After some chitchat, Peter got down to business. "So, guys," he began, "where are we on Otis?"

Jared straightened up, his six-foot five-inch frame towering over the couch and the two line prosecutors flanking him. He opened the bidding. "We've got a strong obstruction case against Emma Simpson, the head of their New York office and one of Otis's top earners, and her deputy, Ben Noguchi. They sent emails telling employees to destroy documents right after we served a grand jury subpoena. Lots of files were deleted from computers and discarded."

He spread his large legs further apart and sat deep into the couch, forging U-shaped impressions in the leather.

Annie moved slightly to her right and burrowed into the corner of the sofa. "Strong" was not the adjective she would have chosen. "Solid," maybe? Or "decent but not a slam dunk"?

McCarthy frowned. "Is that all you've got? Richard Ginsberg is as dirty as a coal mine in West Virginia, and we're no closer to him than we were two years ago?"

This is going to be a long meeting, Annie thought. Jared was turning red as a tomato. Ted was coiled on the edge of his seat, ready to spring forward.

But Weisman shot McCarthy a dismissive glance and cut in first. "C'mon, Mac, we know you've got bigger balls than everyone else. I'd love to get Ginsberg, but we don't have the evidence against him. Not yet, anyway. And the last thing we need right now is a loss in a big case. We can't take the chance."

A voice of reason, finally. Annie leaned forward a little and opened her mouth.

Before she could speak, Ted seized the opening. "Exactly right, Peter. We have lots of smoke, but no witness—not yet." His suit jacket tightened around his broad, muscular shoulders as he spoke. "But I think the obstruction case could be a big step to getting Richard Ginsberg, actually. Right now, Simpson and Noguchi don't think we're serious or that we can nail them. But don't you think she will flip like a pancake if she gets arrested? She's got two teenage kids." He scoffed. "How's her husband going to support that family if she goes to prison? It's not like that winery is profitable."

Great. Let's raise expectations before we've even gotten to the strengths and weaknesses of the evidence, Annie thought. She slumped back into her corner of the sofa again.

Jared nodded. "Ted's right. Simpson is tight with Gins-berg. She could be the key to this."

McCarthy sneered. "That would be great, but what if she doesn't flip? Will Shelby's not going to let her cooperate unless we can really nail her. He's a fighter."

Finally, thought Annie. An opening. She moved forward gingerly and sat up a little higher. "Look, with all due respect, I think we've probably got enough for obstruction. But the case is not open and shut. I'm not sure this woman is going to admit she did anything wrong, and we could lose if she goes to trial."

Peter pursed his lips in a half-sneer. "Okay, look, there's always *some* risk. But it's a pretty good case, right? We serve a subpoena for all sorts of documents. It's clear we're looking at some of their biggest trades. And next thing you know, boom—they're reminding everyone about the," he said, mak-ing rabbit ears with his fingers, "document retention policy."

Ted interjected, "Yeah, and then she even resends the email to remind everyone about how discarding documents is important to protect the company and its employees if there's an investigation or lawsuit. And then, boom, all these documents get destroyed." He rolled his eyes. "Conveniently including tons of analyst notes."

Peter nodded and looked at Annie again. "So, what's the defense? What is *not* open and shut?" He paused and leaned back slightly. "I mean, I get that your buddies here may be a little overoptimistic about the chances of Simpson cooperat-ing. But what's the downside? Why not take a shot?"

Annie resigned herself to her situation. She was not going to win this battle, and this wasn't a hill she wanted to die on. "I hear you," she demurred. "And I actually do think we should go forward. I just want it to be with eyes wide open." Now she had Peter's attention. "She's going to say she didn't know we were investigating Otis itself, never saw the subpoena and thought the investigation was about some stock the people in Boston were trading. That's what Shelby said in his pitch, anyway. And I'm not sure she ever did see the subpoena. It was never emailed to her or anything."

Ted smirked and said, "Even if she never saw it, we've got witnesses who say there was lots of talk about an investigation into Otis all over the New York water cooler when they sent those emails." Weisman nodded. "And there's always the possibility that Ben could flip against her. After all, he's the one who sent the first email. So there's that too."

Overselling again. But at least I tried to lower expectations, Annie thought. *Now the real work is about to start.*

Peter's assistant poked her head into the office and caught his eye. He looked at his watch. "All right, how quickly can you guys get a draft indictment on my desk?"

PART THREE

THE ARREST AND AFTERMATH

CHAPTER 7

THE ARREST

MARCH 13, 2014, 11:00 P.M.

PITCHER LANE, RED HOOK, NEW YORK (DANIEL)

Daniel heard a soft knock on his bedroom door. He quickly turned the phone face down and snuck it under his blanket to obscure the conspicuous blue glow. Then he swiftly grabbed *The Great Gatsby* from his side table and sat up in bed. He turned on the lamp next to his bed and then said, "Mom? Come in. I'm still up."

His mother appeared in the doorway and glanced into the open door to his bathroom as she entered the room. He heard her sigh. *Shit*, thought Daniel, knowing what was coming next.

"I know. I know. I'll pick up the laundry. I promise. Sorry, Mom..." he said sheepishly. As he spoke, her blue-gray eyes warmed up and her face relaxed into a gentle smile as she shook her head softly.

"Yes, that would be nice," Emma said as she approached his bed. "It's getting late, and tomorrow's a school day. You should go to sleep soon. Did you finish all your homework?"

"Um, yeah, just need to read a few more pages for English and then I'll go to bed." Daniel motioned toward the Gatsby book. "By the way, can we go to the DMV so I can get my permit?"

Most of his friends got their permits the day after their sixteenth birthday, and it had already been four months since his. But his parents were so busy, so it just never seemed the right time.

"Sure. Maybe tomorrow afternoon, if I get enough done in the morning." Friday was the day she worked from home. "Did you look through the practice tests?"

"Yes, Mom, of course. I'm ready. Don't worry." Daniel smiled. "Anyway, it's not rocket science, you know."

Emma bent down, flipped her wavy strawberry blond hair out of her face, and kissed Daniel on the cheek. "Okay, I should be able to take you there after school. Maybe I'll even let you practice driving a little on the way home. Good night, little man," she said.

"Good night, Mom. Love you," Daniel replied as she headed toward his bedroom door. He waited until the door clicked shut and then set the book and his phone aside, turned off the light, and fantasized about the possibility of getting his own car—or maybe a truck?—as he drifted off to sleep.

It seemed only minutes later that Daniel heard loud barking and a commotion. He glanced at his clock: 5:00 a.m. At first he just rolled over sleepily, but the noise wouldn't go away. Was it coming from the house? It sounded like Ghost and Dyer were going nuts. He jumped out of bed, his heart racing as he tiptoed to the door and turned the knob slowly, trying to avoid making any noise. Then he heard an unfamiliar male voice. But he couldn't make out what the man was saying, because the dogs were barking so loudly.

Daniel opened his bedroom door and looked down the hall toward the stairway. It was still dark outside, but the light in the front vestibule was on, and the front door of the house was ajar. Daniel saw a round flashing light beyond the open door on the driveway. He could see the back of his father's flame-red hair between the bottom of the stairs and the front door. Dad was still in pajamas. He had his hands up in the air and was walking backward, toward the staircase and away from two strange men in black jackets who were slowly moving further into the house.

Daniel could feel sweat pouring down his neck. His T-shirt was soaked. The dogs were barking at the men menacingly, but not actually trying to attack or bite them. These were Huskies, not toy poodles or dachshunds. Why weren't they doing more? They should be shredding these guys!

Daniel tiptoed to the top of the stairway for a better view, wondering if he should try to get his dad's hunting rifle from the safe in the attic.

Suddenly Daniel heard a click behind him and swung around to find his sister Sarah peeking out of her bedroom. The whites of her eyes were popping out of her head. She ran over to Daniel, and he said, "Shhhh," placing his index finger over his mouth. "Go back to your room," he whispered, waving his hand in the direction of her room. But she was trembling and frozen in place, so he took her hand and pulled her over next to him.

Then one of the men—the shorter one—said to Pierre in a calm but firm monotone: "Sir, calm down. Please get your dogs to back off. We don't want to harm them. And we're not here to hurt you." Then the man said: "We're from the FBI."

Wait, what? What was the FBI doing here at the farmhouse at the crack of dawn? Daniel raised his eyebrows and tilted his head to the side. And now he could see their faces. This guy didn't look old enough to be an FBI agent—in fact, he looked like he could be one of Daniel's tenth-grade classmates.

Then the second guy, who was taller and had a more weather-beaten face, flashed something shiny and pulled out a piece of paper. He showed the paper to Daniel's father and said gravely, "Is Emma Simpson home? We have a warrant for her arrest."

Daniel gasped. His mouth dropped open, and he clapped a hand over it to stay quiet. What was going on? *How could the FBI be arresting Mom, of all people?* he wondered. *She couldn't possibly have done anything wrong.* She obsessed about following the most trivial rules and (unlike Dad) never even got speeding tickets.

He exchanged looks with Sarah and dropped her hand, frozen in place, uncertain what to do next. The rest was a blur. He heard Dad screaming and gesturing at the two of them to go to their rooms. He looked the other way and saw his mother emerging from the bedroom door.

He grabbed Sarah, and they ran back to his room and hid under his covers. He hugged her tightly. They were both trembling, and she started to cry. He took a deep breath and tried to fight back his own tears. He shut his eyes and tried to imagine he was somewhere else—at school, at the gym, riding his bike, anything but this.

This is just a dream, so he could wake himself out of it. Right?

Then he slowly opened his eyes again. It was quieter now. But he was still hiding under the covers with Sarah, who was even wetter than he was. He heard a soft click and then felt the gentle touch of his father, who was shaking like a leaf.

Dad said nothing but slowly lifted the covers, climbed in, and put his arms around them.

* * *

MARCH 13, 2014, 11:00 P.M.

PITCHER LANE, RED HOOK, NEW YORK (EMMA)

After she kissed Daniel goodnight, Emma retired to her bedroom. Pierre was playing "Harvest Moon" on the new Martin guitar she'd just given him for his birthday. She sat on the bed, listening to his mellow, musical voice and tapping her foot to the beat. He had a slight French accent, which still sounded sexy, especially when he sang. He finished the last verse and put the guitar on the stand.

"You want to watch an episode of *The Wire*?" he asked.

Emma and Pierre had started watching old episodes of the show a few weeks earlier. As was typical, once Emma got hooked, if left to her own devices she would binge-watch and speed through entire seasons in days.

Her favorite scene in *The Wire* so far was the one in season one, episode three, when d'Angelo teaches Wallace and Bodie how to play chess and explains that the queen is "smart" and "fierce" and "she's the go-get-shit-done piece." A fitting description of the ideal female, in Emma's mind.

Emma said, "Sure, that sounds good. By the way, Daniel wants to get his permit tomorrow, so I'll try to take him."

Pierre smiled. "Okay, great. Thanks for doing that. It's about time he got it." Pierre switched off the light and turned on the big flat-screen TV on the wall above the fireplace, which glowed with orange flames that warmed the room just the right amount on this cold March evening.

"We're just watching one episode at most. Okay?" Pierre said firmly. "The next one is the finale of season one. We're not going to start a whole new season after we watch it."

"If you insist," Emma said as she climbed under the down comforter on their cherry-wood sleigh bed and snuggled up to his warm body. They watched d'Angelo get sentenced to twenty years—the maximum. She bit her lip as he talked to his mother in prison about how he's got an opportunity to change his life if he cooperates with the federal government in their investigation of the gang.

At this point, Emma glanced over at Pierre, but he was starting to nod off. "C'mon, there's only fifteen minutes left. Let's at least finish the episode," she said.

"Je suis trop fatigué." Pierre sighed.

Emma still liked when he spoke French to her. They had conversed in French a lot in the early years, especially when they first met. Back then, Emma was spending a semester in Paris. These days, it was mostly English. That's what twenty years in the US and having two American children did, she guessed.

Pierre said apologetically: "Sorry. Let's watch the rest over the weekend." He turned off the TV.

Emma groaned. "How can you be so tired? It's only eleven o'clock. And I'm the one who got up at four-thirty this morning." But Pierre wouldn't take no for an answer, so she gave up and kissed him goodnight. She wasn't feeling tired yet, so she grabbed her kindle. A few minutes later, she found herself reading the same line over and over so she closed the cover. Then she too went to sleep.

Only moments later—or so it seemed—Emma was startled out of her slumber by the loud barking of Ghost and Dyer. "What's that?" She sat up in bed, clutching her blanket as tightly as possible. "What time is it? Is someone here? Who would come to the farm at this hour?"

Pierre was already on his way to the bedroom door. He said, "I'll go check. You stay here."

"What if it's an intruder? Should I get the gun from the safe?" Emma wasn't wild about the idea of hiding in the bedroom. She wasn't some helpless female waiting to be saved by her man, was she?

Pierre glanced back at her. The fire had died down, and it was verging on pitch black in the bedroom. "Don't worry," he assured her on his way out. "I'm sure it's nothing—probably just a raccoon or a deer."

"Maybe you're right," Emma mumbled. She sat up in bed for a while, unsure what to do next. The dogs were still barking like crazy.

Screw this, she thought. *Better go help deal with the situation.* She jumped out of bed and dashed out of the bedroom into the second-floor hallway.

Emma was not sure what she had expected, but the sight before her was definitely not it. Just a little further down the hallway, Daniel was crouched down near the floor and peering between the vertical wooden bars of the railing while gesturing toward Sarah, who was approaching him, uncertain what to do. In the living room, the noise from the dogs increased. Ghost's head was down, and he growled but did not attack the two strange men—a short very young one and a taller, middle-aged guy who was trying to speak to Pierre over the cacophony. And beyond the windows, Emma saw a flashing blue light emanating from the roof of some vehicle in the driveway.

Emma darted down the hallway, eager to help Pierre deal with this alarming situation. Just as she was approaching Daniel, however, Pierre emerged at the top of the stairs. The flashing lights lit up his face, which was ashen, his mouth in a tight line.

"Daniel, Sarah, go back to your rooms. *Now!*" he commanded. "I mean it!" *Shit, something must be really wrong if Pierre is yelling*, Emma thought.

The children looked at their mother, their faces stricken with fear, and then immediately scurried back to Daniel's room.

Pierre approached Emma and whispered in her ear: "These men are FBI agents. They say they have a warrant for your arrest and that you need to get dressed so you can go down to court with them."

"What?" Emma's mouth was suddenly wide open, her hands pressed to her cheeks, like the figure in Edvard Munsch's *The Scream*. She said: "That can't be right. My lawyer hasn't heard from the prosecutors in months, and he said they would never charge me without giving him advance warning." The veins in her neck started throbbing. She raised her voice. "How could they do this? I'm going to call Will right now!"

Pierre put his arms around Emma and hugged her tightly, saying, "Listen, everything is going to be all right in the end. We're going to get through this, but we need to be calm…"

The taller agent was starting to walk up the stairs.

"Get dressed. Go with the agents before they start trying to scare the children even more. I'll call Will, and he and I will meet you in court," Pierre said.

"What about the children?" Emma said plaintively.

"Don't worry. I'll take care of them. It's going to be all right," Pierre said, kissing her and then releasing her.

Emma felt like she had just been punched in the stomach while a crane was falling on her head. She lurched back to the bedroom, rummaged in the closet for a few things, and distractedly pulled on a blouse and pants suit.

Will had warned her that the prosecutors were aggressive and could not be trusted. She certainly had moments of anxiety thinking about the investigation from time to time. But in her wildest dreams she never imagined that FBI agents would come to her farm in the middle of the night and arrest her in front of her children—as if she were a violent criminal.

Emma brushed her hair, grabbed a pair of shoes, and grimly made her way back to the landing. The tall FBI agent pulled out a pair of handcuffs, grabbed her arm, and put them on her wrists.

Emma tensed up, unbelieving. "Is this really necessary?" she asked defiantly before remembering Will's warnings not to speak to officers or invite any questions if she was ever approached by the FBI.

"Sorry, ma'am," the agent said, a bit sheepishly. "We have to treat everyone the same; it's protocol."

He led her out of the house and toward the car with the blinking blue light. The sky was still very dark with no hint of the impending sunrise. Suddenly Emma was blinded by LED lights and flashbulbs as the younger agent opened the back door of the police car and motioned for her to get inside.

Emma cast her head downward in shame and urgently ducked into the car to avoid the looming cameras, which seemed to have materialized out of the ether and now disappeared just as quickly into a white van parked across the street.

As the agents slowly drove away, Emma looked down at her lap and noticed that her suit pants were blue, but what was supposed to be the matching jacket was actually gray. She looked back at the house. Pierre was standing in the living room, gazing out the window, watching them drive away.

Things will never, ever be the same again, Emma knew. She closed her eyes as tears streamed down her face, trying not to think about what would happen next.

CHAPTER 8

POST-ARREST
AFTERMATH

———

MARCH 18, 2014

RED HOOK, NEW YORK, 6:30 A.M. (EMMA)

Emma's head was throbbing to the beat of the *thump-thump-thump* of her feet pounding the pavement. She ran north on River Road toward Bard College, pondering her dilemma. It was the first time in five years she'd had time to run on a weekday morning. The orange and purple skies were clear, with just a few cumulous clouds here and there, whitening the colors of the sunrise. The air was still chilly. Emma could see her breath as she aimed for a steady eight-minute mile pace.

She should be enjoying this, but she just couldn't get into it. She didn't belong here, not at this time on this day. She woke up at 4:30 this morning out of habit, unable to go back to sleep. But today, for the first Tuesday in a long time, there was no rush to catch an early train to the city.

The last few days were a total blur. The day of the arrest, of course, was the biggest shitstorm. The morning raid, that interminable ride with the two agents to New York, the "processing" at the FBI building where they took her fingerprints and mug shot. A mug shot! Emma Simpson now had a rap sheet, and whatever happened in this case, she'd always have one.

After the "processing," they took her—in handcuffs—across the street to the federal courthouse, where she waited two hours for a "pre-trial services" officer to ask a bunch of personal questions about her family, her employment, and her finances. None of which was any of their business, of course. But according to Will—who'd finally showed up by that point—she had to answer to get bailed out. After that, she was taken to a cell block in the courthouse.

She sat on a cold stone bench there for four (or was it five?) hours, unable to block out the bright fluorescent light while trying in vain to avoid eye contact with the cast of characters dragged in by the marshals. They looked like they'd come straight off the set of *Law & Order* or *Breaking Bad*. First there were a couple of meth dealers (or rather, alleged meth dealers, she supposed) with tattoos of bare-chested women and crosses. Then there was the Aryan Brotherhood gang member with a shaved head who had been arrested for a dozen home invasion robberies in the Bronx. And, of course, how could she forget the prior felon arrested on a gun charge who kept whistling and blowing kisses at her as she pretended not to notice.

Only later did she realize how parched and hungry she was after so many hours without water or food. She felt like she was shaking the whole time, paralyzed with indecision about whether to inch away as each new denizen was ushered into the area. Or would that just attract more attention? Couldn't they have brought in a nerdy-looking tax evader, or a slick ponzi-schemer, or a books-cooking CEO that day? Or maybe a cybercriminal in a suit? Wasn't this the feds, after all?

All this time in the pens also got her thinking. What if this was her fate? Was she doomed to do time behind bars? Could she survive it? What if she didn't get released today? What if she got convicted and sent away to prison? Who would support the family? Would they have to sell the farm? Would Pierre have to work in the city as a single parent?

The nightmare finally ended—at least for the day—at about four o'clock. They removed the handcuffs and led her in for a mercifully short appearance before a magistrate. After that she was released and driven home by poor

Pierre. He rushed to the courthouse after dropping the kids at school, only to be refused access to her until after the court proceeding.

Emma called the kids from the car and told them she was on her way home. Sarah was relieved but had a million questions: Why was she arrested? Would she have to go to jail? For how long? How could this happen? Emma did her best to sound reassuring, project confidence, and explain that it was all a big mistake.

Daniel was a different story. He refused to get on the call. "Tell Mom I'm busy. I'll talk to her when she gets here," she heard in the background.

When she and Pierre finally arrived home, the pattern continued. Sarah hugged and hugged Emma and seemed not to want to let go.

But Daniel wouldn't come out of his room until dinner was ready. When he emerged, he was sullen. Then came *his* questions: What did you do? Was it insider trading? Why did they arrest you at the house? What will happen to us? Will we have to move away so Dad can get a real job?

She tried the same approach. Pierre backed her up too. But Daniel just glared at her and retreated to his room without even eating dessert.

Then, on Saturday, they had Sarah's final hockey tournament. She was more erratic than usual. She scored a goal but also made several big turnovers. That was unlike her, and the team was eliminated in the first round. Was she distracted, thinking about what happened? And it was impossible not to notice the awkward glances from the other parents or the hushed whispers amongst the opposing team's supporters when they saw her.

What can I do to insulate them from this? It's so awful to think about them suffering because of me, Emma thought as she reached the end of her fifth mile. Her feet moved faster and faster, as if they could somehow outrun her worries. Her pace quickened, closing in on 7:45 per mile.

But her thoughts kept coming back to the situation she faced. Friday and the weekend were bad enough. Just when it seemed things couldn't get any worse, there was Monday, her first day back at the office. When she arrived, she found Richard Ginsberg waiting.

The thought of it set her heart rate into the stratosphere.

Richard, who'd recruited her, had encouraged her to leave Goldman to come in and help build a start-up and was always there for her—apparently until now. He was pale as a ghost and could barely look at her as he spoke. She knew before he opened his mouth that he was bearing bad news. He wouldn't travel down from Boston to tell her he was supporting her through thick and thin, would he? He gazed at the rug, said he was sorry, but he had no choice and had to suspend her immediately.

He sure knows how to kick a dog when she's down, apparently. A pair of dogs, actually. Ben Noguchi was being chucked out too; he'd been arrested while vacationing in Utah with his daughter—also on this ridiculous "obstruction of justice" charge.

At least Richard promised Otis would keep funding the defense and paying Will's astronomical fees. For now, anyway.

Emma picked up her pace as she turned on Budds Corners Road in the final mile of her loop. Her heart was beating fast. The sun was up by now, but Daniel and Sarah would still be at breakfast. What should she tell them? The weekend was difficult enough, trying to reassure them that this was all a big mistake and she wasn't going to prison, that everything was going to be all right in the end. That spiel got a lukewarm response, especially from Daniel. So last night she didn't have the heart to tell them about losing her job.

Maybe she should slow down or walk an extra mile so she could get home after they'd gone to school. Ha! "Disgraced Hedge Fund Star Evades Family Home, Hides from Children." That would make an even better headline than the real one in the *New York Post* on Saturday—"Hedge Fund Hottie Behind Bars." Good thing no one in Red Hook read the *Post*, and Emma's mom lived in Arizona.

Emma breathed hard as she approached Pitcher Lane. At some point, there had to be a conversation and more fallout. Should she keep going straight and delay the inevitable for at least a few more hours or turn left and head back to the farm?

* * *

MARCH 18, 2014

RED HOOK, NEW YORK, 4:00 P.M. (DANIEL)

The sounds of Jay-Z's beat in "99 Problems" pounded into Daniel's ears as he sped down Pitcher Lane on his bike. The cold air grazed his face lightly, but his hood kept the wind at bay as he whizzed down the road mouthing the words to the song. That workout with Ely was fire today. The best part was at the end, when that punk challenged them to a pull-up contest and they kicked his ass.

What flavor shake should I have for today's post-workout? he wondered as he pulled into the driveway and parked his bike.

As he started to open the front door, moving to the beat, the music suddenly stopped. Frowning, he checked his phone. The dreaded empty battery icon. Dead. But the silence was almost immediately shattered by the coffee grinder. Sarah was at lacrosse tryouts, and Dad had a meeting with a supplier in Rhinebeck this afternoon. Who could be home?

Daniel tossed his jacket on the floor and headed to the kitchen. There was Mom, grinding coffee beans. He blinked a few times, but she was still there. Wasn't it Tuesday, though? And this morning she'd been gone by the time he'd had breakfast, as usual.

He froze in the doorway for a moment as reality bonked him on the head. He'd been distracted, daydreaming, not thinking about it. Of course. *She was arrested, wasn't she?* he thought. *She couldn't just go to work as if nothing happened.*

Then he walked over, and the aroma of the grinds wafted over him gently. He loved that smell, even though he didn't really like coffee. But he tried to resist thinking any pleasant thoughts. He wanted answers. He wanted them now.

She said, "Hi," and tried to hug him, but he moved away. She pursed her lips but didn't try again. "How was school?"

"It was okay," he grunted. "But what are you doing here? It's only four thirty." He stared at her. "Did you get fired?" He started assembling the ingredients for his protein shake and put them in the blender.

Emma turned on the coffee maker and sat on a kitchen stool across from him. She looked down for a minute.

"That's it, isn't it?" he said, his decibel rising. "Of course, they had to because you were arrested. Right?"

She put her elbows on the table, rubbed her hands together, and rested her chin on them. Daniel hit liquify on the blender. Through the loud *whir*, he heard her say, "Um, well not fired. But I'm taking a hiatus for a while."

Daniel immediately turned the blender off and sat down across from her. Suddenly he wasn't hungry anymore.

"Did you say 'hiatus'?" He said it slowly, like *hi-aaaa-tussss*. "What does *that* mean?" He rolled his eyes.

"Um, well, it means I can't do my job while the case is happening. I can't work at Otis." She took a deep breath. "So I'll work at home, but mostly on the case. I need to go through the case materials, help my lawyers prepare, stuff like that."

"Are they still paying you? Who's going to support the family if you're not getting paid?"

Emma glanced down again. "Um, well, the truth is…" She sighed, took a deep breath, and slowly looked at him again. The blue in her eyes, often a brilliant azure, had dulled to a grayish slate blue. "The truth is, I'm suspended without pay. They are covering my lawyer's fees, but not my salary anymore."

Fuck, thought Daniel. *This family is* totally *fucked. And what about Mom raising holy hell about my dumb Snapchat messages? As if that was the crime of the century, when she was the one being investigated by feds!*

His blood was boiling as he peppered her with questions. "But don't we need the money? How are we going to pay for stuff? Will we have to sell the farm?"

Daniel could not contain his anger, but he didn't care. He knew Dad made no money from the winery. He had heard him talking about how much he was *paying* to operate it. "And what about college? How are we going to pay for my tuition if you don't have a job?"

Emma crossed her arms and raised her voice slightly. Her tone was firmer now, bordering on defiant. "Listen, don't worry about that stuff. We have lots of money saved up—more than enough for college *and* our expenses for a long time. We're definitely not selling the house. And I'm going to win the case and get my job back," she insisted. "In the meantime, I'll trade our own stock portfolio. I'm pretty good at that, and we'll make plenty of money with investments."

Maybe I'm only sixteen, Daniel thought, *but this is magical thinking. This situation is bad. It's very, very, bad.*

He said angrily: "This is bullshit, Mom. All right? It's not okay that you were arrested, and it's not okay that you lost your job. It's not okay. And pretending it's okay, or that everything will work out somehow, doesn't help."

Then he ran out of the kitchen and out of the house, slamming the door behind him.

He got back on his bike and rode toward Ely's house. *I'm going to hang out there tonight, with a normal family*, he thought.

Fuck this.

CHAPTER 9

PRE-TRIAL PREPARATION (PHASE ONE)

MAY 7, 2014

PITCHER LANE, RED HOOK, NEW YORK

The day started out auspiciously enough. The kids were in a good mood for once and even ate the waffles Emma made for them before jetting off to school. And the weather was finally breaking after several days of nonstop rain and clammy, chilly air that made you feel winter would never end. The sky was a magnificent cerulean hue. There wasn't a single cloud on the horizon. Pink and purple cherry and apple blossoms were popping out all around. The yellow azaleas in the driveway were just about to peak. The scenery was glorious as Emma pulled up to the house after completing today's morning workout, a fifteen-mile bike ride. It was a great way to start the day, even if she planned to spend most of it at her desk.

Emma showered, grabbed coffee and a yogurt, and headed into her home office, the sweet smell of strawberry shampoo still lingering on her big, wavy curls. She spent the morning reading articles about bitcoin and blockchain. She had to do something to keep busy; might as well learn more about these new currencies. Who knew. There was always a chance it could really take off, so why not get in while people were skeptical? The new Ethereum looked particularly interesting as Emma studied Gavin Wood's recently published yellow paper.

She chuckled to herself as she imagined the look on Pierre's face if she told him about this idea. There would be steam coming out of his ears. He'd tell her this was not exactly the best time to gamble on some speculative, new-fangled currency; they should be conserving their resources.

But then again, who was he to question her ideas? What about the winery? Was that little vanity project ever going to turn a profit? Her day trading was more likely to keep the family afloat.

Emma took a deep breath and forced herself to refocus on her investments. She pored over the spreadsheet with their personal portfolio. Surely they could afford to dispose of some of the riskier equities that had done well and move some of the proceeds into Ether. Maybe ten thousand dollars, tops?

Her thoughts were interrupted by an email from Will's associate attaching documents to discuss during their weekly call. Emma sighed and pushed back her chair. The thought of drudging through these emails from two years ago made a trip to the dentist seem appealing. She glanced at her watch. Now was as good a time as any to grab some lunch, wasn't it? This stuff could wait.

Eventually Emma made herself return to her desk. She went through the materials and called Will at the appointed hour.

"Hey, how are you holding up?" Will asked.

"I'm all right, I guess. Could be better, but it is what it is," Emma said. "How's the prep going?"

"Pretty well. We're making our way through the discovery slowly. There's a lot of crap to slog through. But so far, so good. Still haven't found anything we're too worried about," Will said. "We don't see any emails or texts to you about the investigation of the consultant or the subpoena to Otis before you sent your email."

"Yeah, well, you're not going to find any," Emma said, tapping her fingers rapidly on the desk.

"Let me ask you this, though. We won't get statements the witnesses made during the investigation for a while. So we don't know what other people are telling the prosecutors." Will paused for a moment. Then he spoke in an uncharacteristically tentative tone, treading gingerly with his questions. "Uh, do you recall anyone telling you orally about the subpoena? In a meeting or a phone call? Do you think anyone is saying they might have told you?"

Emma's blood was boiling. "Absolutely not. I've told you this before. The only thing I remember hearing—and this was from Doug—was that some consultant the Boston office was using for research on media stocks got a subpoena about Delphun. I had no idea—*no idea*—that there was a subpoena to *Otis* or that the government was asking for any *New York* records.

Dyer walked into the room, sat next to Emma's chair, and looked up at her. She reached down and petted his back, forcing herself to use slow, even strokes.

"Exactly right, exactly right," Will said in a soothing tone. He switched gears. "Take a look at the chronology Josh put together."

Emma opened the document. "Got it."

"So, as you can see, the subpoena to Otis is served on Monday, March twelfth. We don't see any emails to you about it, or telling you to preserve documents, at first. And even after the March fourteenth emails from Ben and you, it is a couple of days before legal tells people to stop destroying documents." Will said.

Emma pursed her lips. She stopped petting the dog and stood up and started pacing. "This is just so random! If we had known there was a broad subpoena to Otis, we never would have sent those emails. None of this would be happening. But now, I could go to jail!" she yelled into the speakerphone.

Dyer stood up and stared at her. He barked a couple of times.

The line went silent for about fifteen seconds. Emma's heart was pounding. Will was always cool as a cucumber. He must think she was a basket case.

"Um, Emma, you're absolutely right to be furious." He rumbled in his baritone calmly. "But their case is crap. You're not going to go to jail. We're going to do everything we humanly can to make sure of that."

Emma closed her eyes, picked up her coffee mug, and slowly took a sip. Then she sat down again, and so did Dyer. "I know. I know, sorry. It just pisses me off." Emma's volume went from eleven back down to five. "Anything else we need to cover today?"

After the call, Emma took the dogs for a one-mile walk to calm herself down, inhaling the sweet smell of the blooming flowers. She surveyed the landscape with its rich palette of green, pink, purple, and yellow vegetation and the occasional decaying red barn, all set off against the polarized blue sky. *Maybe it wasn't all bad, this "working" at home,* Emma thought.

Then the dogs started barking at a jogger who ran by with music blasting out of his headphones. Suddenly Emma remembered that the last time she got a paycheck was two months ago.

She gritted her teeth and headed back to the house to resume her crypto research.

* * *

The rest of the afternoon epitomized the old *Forrest Gump* saw: "Life was like a box of chocolates. You never know what you're gonna get…"

And not in a good way.

As Emma settled back into her home office and started to refocus on the pros and cons of Bitcoin versus Ether, her concentration was shattered by Jimi Hendrix's solo riff on "Purple Haze."

Dyer woke up, rose to his feet, and started frenetically barking. Emma put her finger over her mouth and said, "Shhh, quiet. There's no one here."

Will Shelby's name and photo flashed across her cellphone screen. "Uh, hi," Emma said. Dyer grumbled and lay down again, closing his eyes.

"Hi, Emma. Got a minute?" Will asked.

"Sure, I guess," Emma responded. Hadn't they just spoken? She narrowed her eyes. "What's up?"

She heard Will exhaling. "Look, I have some news." He sounded like Pierre when he went to unclog the toilet because no one else would go near it. "Some unfortunate news," Will continued. "I just got off the phone with Ben's lawyer. Ben has decided to take a plea."

Emma gasped. She was speechless.

"Emma? Are you still there?" Will asked.

Emma's mouth was open, but no words would come out. Finally, she said, very softly, "But why? Why would he do that? He didn't do anything wrong. I don't understand."

"Well, I don't know all the details, of course. Apparently Ben was just too stressed about the risks. With the plea, he has a chance for probation and probably won't get more than six months, maybe a year, tops."

"Six months? A year? In prison?" Emma's voice was shaking. She stood up and started pacing back and forth. "Why? At our last joint defense meeting he was so resolute. He said, 'We're in this together.'" She sank into the lounge chair in the corner. She'd never felt more alone in her life. Ben had always been such a fighter. He'd rather go down in flames than compromise, even over little things.

Will sighed. "It's disappointing. I know. But I guess his daughter is pretty young, and he's got a big mortgage. He didn't want to roll the dice."

"Well, is there any way I can talk to him?" Emma implored. "I mean, I know we're not supposed to talk without our lawyers, but he's one of my best friends. I just want to speak to him about it, even if he's made up his mind." *He's going to say no, isn't he?* she thought, pressing her lips together.

"That's, unfortunately, uh, not a good idea." Will's normally booming voice was quiet. "I know it's a normal human thing to do, but you really shouldn't speak to him, not while the case is ongoing. It could come back to bite you; the conversation could be misconstrued, so..."

Emma suddenly sat up straight, her heart skipping a beat. "Wait, what? Are you saying he's cooperating? Is he throwing me under the bus?" Her voice quavered.

"No, no, no, no," Will said quickly and firmly. "It is a straight guilty plea—meaning he's not testifying against you. Ben wanted you to know he would never do anything to hurt you. He's not going to lie. He would never—"

"Well, won't it hurt me? Won't it hurt me anyway?" Emma interjected. She stood up and resumed her pacing. "Won't the jury find out he pled guilty?"

"No, they won't. It's not admissible; it can't come into evidence under the law," Will explained. "Look, I know you're upset, but—"

Emma stopped pacing and started yelling, "Yes, of course I'm upset! You're damn right I'm upset. He's the one who wrote the stupid email in the first place! None of this would ever have happened if he hadn't. And now he's bailing on me."

Dyer opened one eye and stared at her. Emma realized she was screaming at the phone and sat back down, rested her elbow on the desk, and leaned into her fist. Dyer closed his eye and went back to sleep.

"So, yeah, I'm not exactly peachy keen over here—"

Will breathed loudly again. "Look, who knows. Maybe it's for the best. Sometimes things get messier when you have to coordinate defenses at trial. You do a great cross of some government witness, and then the lawyer for another defendant, instead of leaving well enough alone, insists on trying to put on his own little show. Then before you know it, you're back to square one, and all your careful work is undone. The jury instantly forgets all the great points you made because the witness has managed to muddy things up and back off whatever concessions you got. You can be Perry Mason, but if the other lawyer is My Cousin Vinny, your client is screwed."

Will was getting very animated as he launched into an anecdote about some winnable case he'd lost as a public defender because his client's codefendant had a douchebag for a lawyer.

Then he said, "Anyhow, as you said, he started this. It wasn't even your idea, and it's easier to emphasize that without him at trial." The line went silent for a few seconds. "Try to remember what we talked about earlier. You still have a really strong defense. We can beat this thing."

Emma heard the front door slam, the clink of metal hitting porcelain, and footsteps out in the hallway. Dyer woke up suddenly, jumped up, and ran out of the room, wagging his tail.

"Listen, I've got to go," Emma said. *Gotta stay strong*, she thought. *Gotta be strong. For them.*

"Okay," Will replied. "Hang in there."

Emma stood up slowly and headed out to the front hallway to greet Pierre and Sarah.

* * *

JULY 3, 2014

885 THIRD AVENUE, NEW YORK, NEW YORK

The humidity hung in the air like thick pea soup. Emma trudged through it, feeling like she was on a treadmill to nowhere. Beads of sweat formed a thickening layer over her face and neck. She could see the Lipstick building—and its air-conditioned Shangri-la—protruding out of the urban jungle a mere two blocks away. Yet it seemed a mirage.

She first came to this place for her first meeting with Will exactly a year ago. The weather was the same, but that was about the only thing that had *not* changed.

Emma went from pulling down the big bucks and serving as breadwinner to earning, by comparison, peanuts from very conservative day trading. And when she wasn't trading in what was supposed to be a nest egg, she was exercising outside, helping Pierre with the winery, or trying to find any other distractions that could fill her time and keep her mental health from sinking to new lows. Yet one of those diversions—one of the few she actually looked forward to—was not panning out. Her beloved Yankees were having another crappy year. *Maybe it's time to get rid of Girardi*, she thought.

Her baseball diversion was cut short by a blast of cold air as she moved like lightning through the revolving doors—finally—and on up to the thirtieth floor conference room with its oasis of Fiji water. She was eagerly pouring water into a cup of ice when Will and Josh arrived to greet her.

"How are things?" Will asked. "How's the family?"

"They're okay, I guess. This has been very hard on them, especially Daniel, who is older and more aware of the consequences of this. But we encouraged them to go away for the summer—and hopefully get their minds off the pressures at home and school. Sarah's at a wilderness camp in Maine, and Daniel is a counselor in Colorado," Emma replied.

"That's good to hear." Will took off his jacket and sat down across from her. Josh distributed an agenda. Will peered at it through his matte tortoise shell spectacles. "We've got a lot of ground to cover today. We'll start with an update and then work our way through the rest of these items and any other issues you want to talk about. Okay?" He pushed the paper aside.

"Sounds good." Emma gulped more water and grabbed a napkin to wipe the sweat off her forehead.

"We had a really good conversation with Doug Jones's lawyer, Cristine Kane. I think Doug could be a *very* helpful witness for us."

Emma rested her chin on her hands and leaned forward.

Will sounded animated, as if discovering a good defense witness was like finding a needle in a haystack. "Doug himself never saw the subpoena before you and Ben sent your emails on March fourteenth. He thinks he had heard about it, though he's not sure when. He remembers first learning that one of Boston's consultants got a subpoena and not finding out until a few days later that *Otis* got a subpoena. He thinks Lucy Malomar told him about it, but he's not sure when. And he insists Malomar didn't say anything about the investigators looking into funds managed in New York. He also remembers a staff meeting the morning of the fourteenth—says he brought up the subpoena to the consultant in passing, and that he mentioned it was a Boston issue."

Emma's eyes lit up as she nodded. "That's what I've been telling you. That's what I remember too. He said it was about Boston stuff." She relaxed into her chair. The cool air seemed to have dried the rest of the sweat off her face and neck.

Will leaned forward and smiled as he continued spinning out the story. "There's more. He saw Ben's emails and then yours, and it never occurred to him there was anything wrong with them. He says he probably would've warned employees in New York to preserve documents if there was a subpoena to Otis about the New York office's trades. But he never saw that subpoena until after the shit hit the fan, and the in-house lawyer in Boston sent the firmwide email countermanding your and Ben's emails."

Josh looked up from his notes, glancing tentatively at Will, as if seeking permission to speak. Emma could never figure out why Josh seemed to lack confidence in Will's presence. He had a mind like a steel trap and was the master of the details. Obviously, he didn't have much experience yet, but his questions and comments were usually spot on. *I guess he's a little intimidated and in awe of his boss*, she figured.

Will raised his eyebrows, impatient. "Go ahead, Josh. What've you got?"

"I've gone through Jones's emails, and I don't see any to him with a copy of the subpoena until *after* the fourteenth. We have an email *on the fifteenth* to him with it attached." He showed her a copy. "That means he couldn't have told you what was in the subpoena before you sent your email."

Emma glanced at it. *This is great*, she thought, *but didn't the government know all this? Weren't they supposed to investigate all this before bringing charges?*

She looked up, frowning. "Didn't the prosecutors interview Doug?"

Will sneered in disgust. "He talked to them over a year ago, but it's not clear how much they focused on these topics. They were trying to build an insider trading case, remember? Apparently most of the questions were about compliance practices around potential inside information, use of consultants, and things like that," Will said. "Doug told them his initial understanding was that the investigation was about Delphun trades, but I'm not sure the staff meeting came up or whether they know about that."

Emma shook her head in disbelief. "Well, it doesn't sound like it was very thorough. Maybe I'm being naive, but is there any chance we could use this to persuade them to drop the case?"

Will smirked. "Never gonna happen, especially after Ben's plea. They're dug in. And I don't trust them as far as I can throw them. We can't tip them off about this—much better if it's a surprise at trial."

Emma sighed and said, "I figured you would probably say that. Anyway, he will be a good witness, I think. He's very down to earth, not arrogant at all. Also very lawyerly and precise." She paused. "Could he also be a character witness?"

"Absolutely," Will replied. "He thinks very highly of you, says you were very 'by the book' and insisted everyone attend regular compliance training, et cetera."

Emma took another sip of water. It was icy cold.

"Shall we talk about the jury consultant?" Will asked.

Emma nodded.

"These consultants can often be quite helpful in helping us figure out how to present our themes, what resonates, what's not persuasive, and that sort of thing. In state court cases, lawyers get to ask lots of questions of prospective jurors, and the consultants can be very helpful in figuring out which jurors we should try to keep and which ones to try to keep off the jury. Federal court is a little different. You never get to ask the jurors many questions or learn too much about them."

He took a sip of coffee and continued.

"But good jury consultants can still be really helpful in developing our strategy, getting a sense of how different arguments may play with potential jurors of different backgrounds. For instance, we often run focus groups. The consultant recruits people from the jury pool to participate; they watch a mock trial we put on and then break up into groups to 'deliberate.' We can watch and listen to their conversations to see what real people think of the arguments. It's quite interesting, and sometimes surprising, how people react. The person I have in mind is Akiko Davis. I'll bring her in next time we meet."

"That sounds great, but I've heard jury consultants are really expensive. Are you sure Otis will pay for it?" Emma asked. There was no way she would even think about dipping further into their slowly dissipating savings to pay for her defense costs. How would they pay off the debts on the winery? So far, the company had not complained about Will's bills, but they hadn't been that high—yet. "If the defense costs get crazy, maybe they'll stop paying, right? Things have been tough after the redemptions last year."

"Actually, the General Counsel has already approved my proposed budget for this. I think they are still very supportive, at least as to this. They do want you to win the trial, you know," Will replied.

Emma rolled her eyes.

Will flashed a sheepish half-smile. He said, "I know you're still angry about how they treated you after the arrest, but no company in the financial industry can keep someone on in this situation. Trust me."

A staffer entered the room and laid out sandwiches, salads, and snacks on the side table next to the remaining Fiji bottles.

"Let's take a short break and grab some lunch. After that, we're going to have you take us through your daily routine at work in more detail—what you focused on, things like that, and what you did at work on March fourteenth—to help us start crafting how we tell the story to the jury." Will pointed to the two large binders next to her.

"Great," Emma said, "although this might just put you to sleep." She took a deep breath and settled in for what sounded like a long afternoon.

It all seems like ancient history at this point, Emma thought as she tried to visualize her office and her former work life in order to describe it to the lawyers.

She was thoroughly exhausted by the time they closed the second binder. A long day of a very different type of work, Emma thought wistfully. But, she guessed, a pretty productive one.

And with Doug in her corner, maybe, just maybe, there was some light at the end of this long, dark tunnel.

CHAPTER 10

PRE-TRIAL PREPARATION (PHASE TWO)

—

SEPTEMBER 27, 2014

It was Friday night, and Emma's trial was less than two months away. Will was already deep into trial prep, but at least he still had time to relax a little on weekends. Hopefully tonight he could enjoy a nice dinner with Nia at Franco's, an Italian Restaurant around the corner from their apartment on East End Avenue. They'd reserved tickets to *The Dark Knight Rises* too. Will wasn't a huge fan of superhero movies—that was more of a Nia thing—but he'd enjoyed the first two in this series, so why not indulge her?

Will went into the small family room and bent down to kiss his two young sons, who were playing with the babysitter. "Have fun, guys. Don't do anything I wouldn't do." He winked. "Mom and I are heading out now."

Nia was already waiting for him in the front hallway. As they walked over to the restaurant, she said, "Man, what a great day. Mike was so relieved to get probation. We really thought the judge was going to make him do at least *some* time because the government asked for three years! It's great to feel like you can help someone—a real human—with a big problem." She grinned. "I'm so glad I finally left the US Attorney's Office when I did."

Will laughed. "Well, you've changed a lot since the Federal Defender told me in my interview that he was in the middle of a fight with you about whether some dude should get twenty years for illegal reentry."

"That was a really bad guy! He had a long rap sheet stacked with armed robberies and shootings," Nia insisted.

"Well, my current client isn't a bad guy, as you know. And I was hoping I could pick your brain about an issue in the case," Will said. "It'll be quick, I promise, and then we can talk about something more fun."

"Okay," Nia said, "but only if you'll share the burrata and prosciutto with me."

Will frowned. "Fine, but just this once, or I'll have to skip my 'rest' day and double my workout time at the gym this week. You don't want me losing my six-pack, do you?"

Nia rolled her eyes.

"So here's the deal," he continued. "Remember how I told you that when Emma was arrested, a *Wall Street Journal* reporter and two photographers were waiting outside her house? And we think the FBI or someone at the US Attorney's Office tipped off the press?"

Nia nodded.

Will continued: "Well, now I think we know who it was. Believe it or not, Peter Weisman himself—"

He stopped speaking as Giovanni, Franco's owner, approached them from inside the tiny restaurant. He didn't want anyone to hear this, especially not Giovanni, who was a huge gossip.

Giovanni was a thin, silver-haired character with a slight Northern Italian accent. He dressed casually and always wore a Patagonia vest. He delighted in playing maître d', regaling his guests with where the ingredients for his daily specials came from, how his alleged restaurant in Rome was doing, and his thoughts on the latest disasters befalling his favorite New York sports teams, especially the hapless Knicks.

"How many tonight? Just two? Left the kids at home, I see," Giovanni said as he approached Will and Nia. They were standing outside the tiny restaurant, which could barely squeeze in twenty small tables and the large pizza-oven in the back. "Give me about ten minutes, and I can get you into one of the tables in the back." Giovanni motioned toward a table for two right next to the brick oven. "By the way, how's that case with the hedge-fund lady going?"

"We're getting ready for the trial. It's going to be tough. There's already been a lot of bad publicity," Will said. He hesitated to volunteer more, wondering what was coming next. Giovanni could be hilarious, but he was kind of a loose cannon.

Giovanni grinned and said, "Don't worry. You're going to win. You know, the DA told me he knows she's innocent, but he's just trying to bust her chops to teach her a lesson..." Then he got distracted because one of the waiters was waiving him over to a table where people needed a wine recommendation. "Back in a few," he said and walked off.

Nia looked at Will. She laughed after she was sure Giovanni was out of earshot and said: "Like we're supposed to believe he really spoke to one of the AUSAs about this? I don't even think they live around here or would ever come to this restaurant. Doesn't Ted live in Brooklyn Heights?" She shook her head. "Anyway, how do you know Weisman is the leaker? I guess it's not surprising, though it's outrageous. When I was in the Office, it was different. My boss would never have done something like that. At the very least I would have thought he'd try to cover his tracks more carefully."

"Yeah," replied Will. "I'm sure he *is* super careful. But you know, you don't get so many puff pieces written about you unless you're putting out to the media. Anyway, remember how a few months ago we were having drinks in mid-town after work and we saw Weisman there with a mysterious woman?"

Will smirked as Nia laughed.

"Anyway," Will said, "I found out who she was. Janet Seagram, the *Wall Street Journal* reporter who covers these insider trading cases! Can you believe that? No wonder the *Journal* was tipped off in advance about the arrest."

Will's face tensed up.

"It just pisses me off. They wouldn't give us the courtesy of letting her surrender—a mother of two, no prior history of even so much as a speeding ticket. And all so they can leak to the media to orchestrate this ridiculous perp walk." Will glanced around and dropped his voice. "But is there anything we can do with this? I want the judge to know about it. It's obviously misconduct, but I really don't see a viable motion. Do you?"

"Sorry, babe," Nia replied. "Nothing you can do with this, unfortunately, I don't think. I wouldn't even tell Emma about it. That will just set her into orbit, sending you on tangents that will get nowhere. Just focus on the trial. You've got such a strong case, and she's that rare client who could be a great witness if she testifies."

Just then, Giovanni waved them into the restaurant and ushered them to the back table he had promised.

"So, Giovanni, what are tonight's specials? Promise me you have the burrata since I actually got him to agree to share it." Nia winked at Will conspiratorially.

Giovanni put his thumbs inside the armholes of his vest and started going through his spiel, talking a mile a minute about the intricacies of the various dishes and their provenance.

Will didn't try to keep up with his rapid-fire patter. He was going to just order the chicken dish he usually chose anyway, so his thoughts wandered back to the case.

Nia was probably right, but he was still seething over Weisman's obsession with media coverage and staging that perp walk. Best not to think about it anymore, at least for now, when he still had a few hours here and there to think about something other than the upcoming trial.

* * *

OCTOBER 31, 2014

500 PEARL STREET, NEW YORK, NEW YORK

When Will entered the courtroom for the final pre-trial conference, he was full of energy. The sun was shining outside, and the windows on either side of the bench lit up with a soft golden glow. Even that odd red and blue piece of woven tapestry on the wall between the two windows looked vibrant. And, for the first time in weeks, it was sixty degrees out. The end of Emma's long ordeal seemed just around the corner with the trial coming up.

Mrs. Vappur, the courtroom deputy, smiled as she called the case.

Judge Robert Gregory himself, however, did not look so chipper as he slowly made his way to the bench. "All right, counsel, I've got a sentencing shortly, so we need to get through these evidentiary issues quickly. Let me hear from the government first," he growled, looking at Ted Hardin. He always looked at Ted.

But Annie Waters stood up instead and walked to the podium. She looked striking in her slate green pantsuit and flashed her matching hazel eyes at the judge. *Maybe the judge will notice her now*, Will mused.

"Your Honor," Annie said in her most earnest, mellifluous voice, "we've made two motions. First, we're seeking to introduce charts showing Simpson's compensation in 2010 and 2011. This is evidence of her motive to obstruct justice when she sent the email. She made seven million dollars and ten million dollars in those years and had a lot to lose if the fund or its employees were prosecuted for insider trading."

She paused for effect.

"Second, we seek admission of evidence showing background, the suspicious Otis trades the government was investigating. These trades are highly relevant because they show the defendant's motive to hide evidence of serious crimes."

"I've read your papers," Judge Gregory said impatiently.

Not a good sign. *Sounds like he's already made up his mind,* thought Will. *Why do judges always allow them to poison the well like this?* It seemed like in every white collar case the first thing the prosecutors wanted to tell the jurors was that the defendant had more money than they did.

Then the judge said: "Let me hear from Mr. Shelby. Why shouldn't I grant the government's motions?"

Will slowly rose and stood to his full height, hoping his deliberate style could slow things down and capture His Honor's attention. He looked at the judge intently.

"Let me start with the compensation. It's not relevant at all, but it is highly prejudicial. Ms. Simpson was well compensated, as most successful hedge fund managers are. By contrast, most of the jurors make far less money. It's highly inflammatory—"

"I make far less money too," the judge interjected, grinning as he glanced toward the reporters at the back of the courtroom. The audience laughed. Will smiled and tried to conceal his irritation.

Always playing to the press, isn't he? Will thought.

Then Will said: "In all seriousness, Judge, Ms. Simpson worked very hard to get to her position. The fact that she was so successful is hardly a motive to obstruct justice. There's zero evidence she ever had anything to hide when it came to this insider trading investigation. Zero evidence that destroying documents would have protected her compensation or that not destroying them would have risked a penny of it.

"And, as the cases we've cited demonstrate, a wealthy person doesn't have any more incentive than a poor person to break the law to protect her job. But there's a huge risk of unfair prejudice. And the Supreme Court and the Second Circuit have held that appealing to class prejudice is highly improper and cannot be condoned."

Judge Gregory sneered as he shot a glance at Emma. She was dressed in a smart designer suit and wearing a beautiful set of pearls.

Shit, thought Will. *We told her to be careful not to wear jewelry in front of the jury, but who would have thought this was an issue with the judge? Too much time on a government salary, I guess.*

"Well, I don't think anyone is trying to inflame the jury. Surely you're not suggesting Ms. Waters is trying to start a class war here," the judge said, again drawing laughter from the gallery. "I'll allow it."

He paused and looked at his notes.

"What about the evidence of the insider trading? Why isn't that relevant background?"

Will clenched his jaw and gripped the podium tightly as his temperature rose. He was tempted to say, "It's about as relevant as her salary," but resisted the impulse. Instead, he said, "For several reasons, Your Honor. First and foremost, there *was no evidence of insider trading.* Not a shred. The government was never able to prove *any of the trades* they want to tell the jury about were based on insider information. All they can show is that these were profitable trades, and the funds made money from them. So what? Is it now criminal to make money from investing in stock?"

Judge Gregory interrupted again. "Well, if you say the evidence doesn't prove insider trading, how is it prejudicial? You can just argue to the jury that the trades aren't illegal."

"But, Judge," Will said, raising his voice slightly, now unable to conceal his frustration. "Then we're going to have a mini-trial on that subject, which is totally irrelevant. The government couldn't make an insider trading case, so now we're here on this email. That's the charge. That's what the case is about. Did Ms. Simpson send the email because she was trying to get people to destroy documents responsive to the subpoena, or was it innocent? If you let them introduce innuendo about insider trading, it's going to confuse the issues, distract the jury, and create a wildly prejudicial and unfair impression that Otis is a corrupt company and that people who work there a propensity to commit crimes. These are exactly the types of unfair effects the Rules of Evidence are intended to prevent." His face felt flushed.

"Well," said Judge Gregory, "I certainly don't want a mini-trial, so any evidence about this will have to be very limited." He looked at Ted again, as if to signal he was sure Ted somehow would be responsible about this and wouldn't play it to the hilt.

What a joke, Will thought. *Tails they win, heads we lose.*

Then the judge said, "But I will allow some very limited evidence of trades the government thinks are suspicious. Is there anything else I need to take up today?" Hearing no response, Judge Gregory motioned to Mrs. Vappur to call the next case.

Will stood up and put his hand gently on Emma's shoulder. She looked like she had been hit by a Mack truck. Will, for his part, felt like Michael Spinks right after his fight with Mike Tyson. That one took only ninety-one seconds but still felt the same as the ten minutes he just fought in front of—or really with—the judge.

As Will left the courtroom, his shoulders slumped. Hands in his pockets, he couldn't stop thinking about how he was going to explain what just happened to Emma. He was so naive when her case was assigned to this judge. He did know, of course, that it was going to be a problem, but he never imagined just how bad things could get.

He often told clients that there were three kinds of judges in the Southern District of New York: a few who were unfailingly pro-government and would almost never rule in favor of a defendant on any issue, big or small; a few who were sometimes fairly skeptical of the government and were the best draws for a criminal defendant; and the rest of the bunch, who probably unconsciously leaned in favor of prosecutors but tried hard to be fair and would generally at least hear you out.

Judge Gregory was definitely in that first group, but he wasn't a draconian sentencer, and some other judges seemed even worse. Gregory had been a prosecutor in the US Attorney's Office in Manhattan for ten years before taking the bench. He'd mostly worked on organized crime cases and prosecuted violent bad guys, and he had no other experience to speak of apart from a couple of years as a young associate pushing paper at a Wall Street law firm. He never represented an individual client, which was not helpful.

Still, Will thought maybe he would be better in a weak white collar case. You would think someone who prosecuted serious violent crime would be unimpressed by a thin case based on nothing but a short email like this.

But even if that turned out to be wishful thinking, never in his wildest dreams could Will have imagined the tsunami now drowning the defense.

PART FOUR

THE TRIAL

CHAPTER 11

THE TRIAL (OPENING STATEMENTS)

NOVEMBER 4, 2014

500 PEARL STREET, NEW YORK, NEW YORK

Emma sat behind the long wooden table in the back of the well of the large wood-paneled courtroom. Barriers on every side penned her into her little corner of the cavernous arena: a big table in front of her separating the prosecutors from the defense; a birch-colored railing behind her shielding the audience from the parties; on her left, her lawyer's big chair, and, to her right, the jury fenced into their little rectangular wooden box.

Emma stared at the empty yellow pad in front of her and tapped her pencil on it repeatedly. She felt numb and disconnected from her surroundings. It was as if she had just discovered she'd been living in a simulation for the past forty-five years with no ability to control a destiny that was simply the product of algorithms in someone else's computer program.

What was she doing here? Every morning for the past six months, she would wake up and think, for just a minute, that this was only a nightmare that must have ended with the rise of the morning sun or the jolt of her alarm clock going off. But then, almost immediately, she would see or hear something that brought her back to the truth about what was happening to her.

This morning, reality set in before Emma had even a glimmer of hope of escaping her nightmare because she woke up in unfamiliar surroundings—a room in a small but trendy hotel on West Broadway in lower Manhattan, about five blocks from the federal courthouse. Sometimes it seemed the lawyers could get more done without her around as they prepared their cross-examinations and the opening statement and wrote their motions on evidentiary disputes. But they insisted she stay in the city on trial days to work out of their "war room" in the evenings. They wanted her to help with facts, and they had to prep her for her likely testimony. They wouldn't make a final decision about whether she would take the stand until the government rested its case, but she had to be ready. Emma couldn't imagine not testifying, anyway.

It was just as well. Commuting back and forth on trial days would have been too much of an emotional whipsaw between her two worlds—home with family and the lush flora and fauna of Red Hook versus this surreal combat in the bowels and grit of Gotham. The clean but anodyne hotel room, with its Scandinavian furniture in hard-edged lines, its soft mattress, its charcoal-gray walls, its "view" of Starbucks and a nearby bodega, and its honking cars, only made the current situation worse—if that was even possible.

Emma missed Pierre's morning coffee, the firm mattress and cozy surroundings of her farmhouse bedroom, and the fact that the only early morning sounds there were the chirping birds. And she really missed Daniel and Sarah and Pierre—even if sometimes it felt as if all her interactions with Daniel devolved into arguments. He seemed like he was blowing off his schoolwork, doing the minimum necessary, as if he could somehow charm and BS his way to decent grades like he did in middle school.

It was hard enough to strike the right balance as a parent. She didn't want to be on his case all the time, because that would surely backfire. On the other hand, a laissez-faire approach would inevitably make matters worse. And on the third hand, even timid attempts to ask whether homework was completed or whether he was studying for an upcoming test were met with outbursts and sarcastic rejoinders—"What difference does it make? I don't really want to go to college anyway," or, "What, so I can end up like you? Why would I want that?"

Now, sitting at the counsel table beside her lead lawyer, Emma was startled out of her detached state by two loud knocks emanating from a large door near the empty bench in front of the courtroom. Will nudged her. Then she stood up as Judge Gregory emerged from the door in his black robes. He walked slowly toward the steps elevating the bench from which he would preside over her trial. It was only a short distance from the door to the steps, but far enough to reveal that—particularly in comparison to the lanky young law clerk holding the judge's papers—His Honor was a man of short stature but considerable girth.

Judge Gregory ambled over to the bench and then looked down at the prosecutors and Agent Marsh, who were sitting at the front counsel table. "Good morning, everyone. Please be seated. I'm told all the jurors are here, so I'd like to get started right away with opening statements."

He leaned down and whispered something to the courtroom deputy, who was sitting just below him. She had coal-black hair, always made jokes outside his presence and seemed friendly—and human—in stark contrast to the dour-faced Judge. But her hands looked gnarled and arthritic. *She must be a lot older than she looks and acts*, Emma thought.

Mrs. Vappur told the Marshal to bring in the jurors, and everyone stood up again as they entered the courtroom and took their seats in the jury box. Emma's stomach was churning as she scanned their faces slowly. Jury selection was a blur; it went by so fast. There was no time to learn much of anything about the jurors, and they had almost no control of who made the panel. But one thing was crystal clear. This was hardly a jury of her peers. Only four jurors had a college degree, and two of those four seemed openly hostile to hedge funds and people who worked on Wall Street. She held her hands behind her back, cracking her knuckles until she realized what she was doing and forced herself to stop.

During jury selection one juror, a twenty-somethingish woman who worked at MSNBC's *Rachel Maddow Show*, was staring fawningly at prosecutor Ted Hardin. She whispered conspiratorially with an unemployed young man who himself was apparently captivated by the perfect geometry of Annie Waters's face and her fetching hazel eyes. Another juror was an older, self-professed "democratic socialist" from Greenwich Village, who said she believed "greedy bankers" were ruining the American economy. Of course, she insisted she could be fair and decide the case based on the evidence, so Judge Gregory rejected the defense efforts to strike her for cause.

On the other hand, a few jurors seemed to offer a ray of hope. There were two middle-aged, hard-working Black men (one worked for the Metropolitan Transit Authority, the other owned a small hardware store). They were the only Black jurors and were constantly yukking it up together. They appeared to be potentially sympathetic. Each of them had smiled at her, and the MTA guy nodded when the judge was explaining the presumption of innocence during the preliminary instructions. The hardware store guy even said he had been stopped by the police several times for no good reason but could be fair to the government; hopefully he was at least willing to hear both sides of the story.

Emma was surprised the prosecution hadn't struck that man. Will told her it was probably because they only had a limited number of challenges, which they used to strike several corporate lawyers, a business school professor, a staffer for a Republican state legislator, and two investment bankers—basically, all the well-educated people who didn't have some perceived ax to grind against the financial industry or successful securities traders.

Emma turned her gaze back toward Judge Gregory as he greeted the jurors and told them it was time for opening statements. "Government, are you ready?" he asked the front table.

"Yes, Your Honor." Emma saw Ted Hardin stand up, button his well-tailored cobalt suit jacket, and take a few long strides to the podium. *Wait*, she wondered, *doesn't he have any notes?* He didn't have anything in his hands. How could he not even need notes?

Emma glanced quickly to her right at the table surface in front of Will. She saw several piles of handwritten notes and his thin black binder, which she knew contained his opening, meticulously typed in fourteen-point font. She frowned. Is he ready for this? He was brilliant and seemed polished when he practiced his opening last night. But every now and then, he reminded her a little of those absent-minded professor types.

Emma suddenly remembered Will's instructions not to show emotion or concern to the jurors. She reverted to her poker face and turned her attention back to Hardin.

He put his hands on the podium, paused, and looked intently at the twelve jurors and two alternates seated in front of him. "Good morning, ladies and gentlemen. This case is about one woman's effort to obstruct justice and destroy evidence. It's about how a powerful and successful Wall Street hedge fund manager tried to interfere with a federal investigation—an investigation looking to see whether her business was violating laws to protect investors in the stock market. An investigation to see if her company was cheating and trading on inside information to get an edge ordinary investors have no access to. This woman seated at the second table—Emma Simpson—"

Hardin dramatically pointed straight at Emma. She knew this was coming but wasn't prepared for just how creepy it made her feel. She wished she could put on an invisibility cloak. She tried not to squirm, putting her hands underneath her thighs. Then she deliberately looked away from Hardin and turned toward the jury. She softened her mouth and flashed a soft, inviting gaze at them, begging them to see her as a real person, a good person, not the caricature he was trying to paint. Most of them responded with poker faces, but the transit worker caught her eye, smiled slightly, and then looked back at Hardin.

Hardin disregarded Emma and resumed his story. "Emma Simpson *knew* that the federal government was investigating her company's stock trades. And knowing that this investigation threatened her business, her reputation, and her career, she told all the people who worked for her to destroy their notes and other documents about why they traded certain stocks, so federal investigators wouldn't be able to see what was in those files. She told those people to destroy documents a federal grand jury had demanded to see and had a right to see."

Emma twisted her wedding ring and looked down at the note pad in front of her. When would this be over? Would he ever stop talking? For a fleeting moment, she imagined herself standing up, dashing out of the courtroom, jumping into the elevator, and bolting out of the building.

Then she took a deep breath and forced herself to return to reality.

Hardin's voice rose as he said: "Emma Simpson's effort to obstruct justice was a serious federal crime, and that's why we are all gathered here today in this courtroom..."

* * *

For the next thirty minutes, Emma sat in her chair, looking straight ahead and hearing but not really listening as she tried to shield herself from the torrent of arrows, darts, bullets, and grenades being slung in her direction. She kept a stony face and erect posture.

Finally, mercifully, Hardin wound up his opening, saying: "This is a very important case. It's important to the United States because we all have a strong interest in enforcing the laws intended to protect the federal government's investigations. And it's important because obstruction of justice is a serious federal crime. Now, I'd like to ask you to do three things during this trial: listen to the evidence, follow the law, and use your common sense."

He paused and raised his voice, ever so slightly, as he looked intently at the jurors, who all returned his gaze attentively.

"If you do those three things, there is only one fair verdict: Emma Simpson is *guilty*." He paused and then slowly walked from the podium back to his seat at the prosecution table.

Emma felt a pit in her stomach as she reviewed Hardin's rapt audience of jurors. They were definitely listening. On the other hand, she thought, maybe it's just because they took this seriously. It would probably be much worse to have bored or sleepy jurors. Wouldn't it? But will they keep paying attention? The Maddow lady whispered something to her new boyfriend, who nodded and gave her a knowing smirk.

Judge Gregory suddenly noticed the silence and glanced up from his computer screen. It was hard to tell if he was doing other work, playing solitaire, or watching YouTube videos without the sound.

The judge saw that Hardin was seated again, so he nodded at Emma's attorney. "Mr. Shelby, you may proceed."

Will stood up, smoothed over his charcoal gray suit pants, adjusted his John Lennonish glasses, and walked over to the podium. His stride was silky smooth, and his lanky frame made him look somewhat taller than his actual height of six feet, two inches. The pit in Emma's stomach receded somewhat as she felt a ray of hope watching the strikingly handsome Will, as all eyes in the courtroom turned his way. Will put his thin black binder on the podium, opened it up, and fixed his deep brown eyes on the faces of the jurors.

His voice had a resonant bass tone that boomed throughout the cavernous courtroom. No microphone needed. "Good morning. I'd like to start by taking you to the scene of the crime, the room where it happened." He articulated the words slowly, with just a tiny, barely perceptible hint of sarcasm and a very somber face. "This is it, ladies and gentlemen, right here…"

Will paused and then pointed to his left as a photo of Emma's iPad suddenly appeared on the large flat-screen monitor and then slowly morphed into a blown-up version of her March fourteenth email. "What is this case about? It's about a three-line email Emma Simpson sent at the end of a long, busy day on her way home to her family."

The text Emma had typed above Ben's email message to the New York office was highlighted in yellow, as if by magic, as Will spoke. The jurors turned their eyes to the screen and then back to Will as he continued speaking.

"A three-line email sympathizing with her colleagues' frustrations about the disruptions that would be caused by computer upgrades, and confirming a colleague's suggestion to follow company procedures about documents to get ready for these upgrades," Will said. "Now, what you are going to learn during the course of this trial is that this email is *exactly* what it says it is." He paused for a moment and then continued his slow, resonant delivery: "This email is an endorsement of Ben Noguchi's recommendation to follow company policy and help reduce document clutter before a new computer system is installed. It is nothing more and nothing less. And it is *certainly* not a federal crime."

Even the Democratic Socialist seemed caught in his spell, unable to take her eyes off Will. She was on the edge of her seat, drinking in every word.

"The story of this three-line email, in fact, is a very simple one," Will explained. "I am going to give you a preview of that simple story and suggest that as you listen to the testimony, you focus on one basic question.

The email disappeared from the screen, and the white background on the large TV screen was filled with a bullet that said, "What was Emma Simpson's intent?"

Will read it aloud and paused. "This is really the key to this case. What was Emma Simpson thinking when she sent this email? What was in her head? Was she thinking about the government's investigation into Otis? Did she even know that the government was investigating Otis, as opposed to some consultant at another company? What did she know about any investigation when she sent the email? Did she know there was a subpoena to Otis? Did she see any subpoena to Otis before she sent the email?"

He looked intently at the jurors. "As you listen to the evidence and think about this question, ask yourself: Is there anything fishy or suspicious about asking people to clean up their files before the transition to a new computer system? Was the computer upgrade in the works before anyone heard about the investigation, or did someone decide to do it as a pretext for destroying documents? You will learn that it was planned far in advance and was always scheduled for roll-out in late March. And ask yourself: Was the company policy attached to the email unusual or suspicious? Was it new? Was it designed for a bad purpose?"

He paused for a moment, as if waiting for the jurors to answer, and then said: "No, you will learn, it had been in place for years. And it was a fairly standard, commonplace policy, reflecting good record-keeping practices. In fact, many businesses have these types of policies."

Emma's jaw clenched and her shoulders tensed up. Then she forced her face to relax, dropped her shoulders and sat up a bit straighter in the large, uncomfortable wood and leather chair. The juror who worked for the Maddow show glanced over at Emma. Was that a smirk, or was Emma imagining that?

Will seemed to notice the Maddow lady looking askance, so he focused his eyes like a laser-beam directly at her. She immediately turned her attention back to him, like a kid caught with her hand in the cookie jar.

Having retrieved his audience, Will resumed speaking, his cadence rising as he warmed to his themes. "Was Emma Simpson thinking about an investigation, was she worried about a federal case against Otis? Not at all." Then he repeated himself, elongating the words: "Not. At. All. In fact, Emma didn't even know that Otis had been served with any subpoena. She certainly didn't know investigators were looking for any documents in Otis's New York office. She barely knew there was an investigation. She wasn't thinking about any investigation. She was doing something she often did. She was trying to generate support for a company initiative—the computer upgrade—and backing up a colleague who suggested employees follow good business practices."

Will looked intently at a zaftig forty-somethingish waitress of Russian descent. She seemed a bit of a cipher during jury selection but now was nodding as Will said, "In fact, she wasn't thinking much about this at all. It probably took her thirty seconds to send this during a very busy day—a day in which she woke up at four thirty in the morning, traveled one hundred miles from her home to the office, spent hours in meetings, and then rushed out to get home to dinner with her husband and two children..."

Hearing this, the hardware store owner—he said he had children, didn't he?—slowly looked over at the prosecution table. A good sign, possibly? Was he perhaps wondering why they'd made a federal case out of a three-line email? Or was he tiring of Will's opening and getting distracted? A chill came over Emma suddenly, and she crossed her bare legs to warm them up.

About fifteen minutes later, Will completed his opening. As he shut his black binder and strode back to the defense table, Emma slowly closed her eyes for a minute, as if doing so might transform this experience into a dream and help her wake up to a sunny new day on the farm.

But then she heard Mrs. Vappur say, "All rise." Emma opened her eyes, stood up, and watched Judge Gregory descend from the bench while the jurors filed out.

CHAPTER 12

PROSECUTION'S CASE (I)

NOVEMBER 5, 2014

500 PEARL STREET, NEW YORK, NEW YORK

Fifteen hours later, Emma was back at her spot in the packed courtroom.

Annie Waters rose from her seat and announced, "The government calls Lucy Malomar."

Malomar, a petite woman in her mid-thirties who could easily have been mistaken for a model if she'd been just a few inches taller, emerged from behind the well. She was immaculately dressed in a dove gray Tahari suit, a pink Hermes scarf with turquoise fish on it, and long black leather Botticelli boots that draped her sleek calves. Her mane of coal-black hair was neatly fixed in place by a maroon silk headband; not a strand stood out of place. She strode slowly toward the stand, looking straight ahead, and took her seat and her oath. She gazed directly at Waters.

Why won't she look at me? Emma thought. *Not a good sign.*

"Ms. Malomar, where do you work?" Waters asked.

"I am an Associate General Counsel of Otis Capital," Malomar said.

"What are your responsibilities as Associate General Counsel?"

Malomar said quietly, "I help our General Counsel develop policies and procedures to ensure that we comply with legal and regulatory requirements established by the SEC and other government agencies. I review our disclosures to investors and provide advice to analysts and traders about securities regulations on an as-needed basis. I'm also responsible for managing any litigation for our company."

"In 2012, did Otis have a document retention policy?" Waters asked.

"Yes."

Waters handed Malomar a document, which was admitted into evidence.

"What's the purpose of this document?" Waters asked.

"It describes the company's policies regarding document creation and retention," Malomar replied.

"What does it say employees should do if there is litigation or a subpoena?"

Malomar flipped through the document and looked up. "If an employee learns of litigation involving the company or the existence of a subpoena, the obligation to comply with this policy is suspended—meaning documents may not be discarded or destroyed once the employee learns of that information."

Waters asked, "How did Otis make sure employees knew about this policy?"

"Well," Malomar continued, "everyone was given a copy of the policy, and we had training about it. So if a person learned of a subpoena or litigation, from whatever source, they were required to retain documents."

Emma clenched her teeth. *Why did she have to volunteer that last sentence?* She tried to catch Lucy's eye. But Lucy kept her tunnel vision fixed on Waters.

"Did there come a time when you learned of an investigation into possible insider trading at Otis?" Waters asked.

"Yes, in early March 2012," Malomar responded. "At first, all I knew was that a consultant working with one of our portfolio managers had received a subpoena from the US Attorney's Office."

"Did you share that information with anyone in Otis's New York office?"

"Yes," Malomar said. "I believe I mentioned it during a call with Doug Jones, who is in our legal department and works in New York. I told him we weren't too sure what the government was investigating, or whether it might affect Otis, but that this consultant was someone our media team used for investment research. And I told him we believed the subpoena concerned a company called Delphun Media."

"When was that phone call with Mr. Jones?" Waters inquired.

"It would have been within a day of learning about the investigation, I believe," Malomar replied. "So sometime in the first week of March."

"Why did you share this information about the investigation with Mr. Jones?"

Will stood. "Objection."

Judge Gregory looked up from one of his computers. He glanced at his other screen, which Emma was told had a real-time transcript on it.

Great, glad he's paying attention, she thought, rolling her eyes in her mind.

"Overruled," the judge said. "You may answer."

Malomar looked up at the judge and then back at Waters. "I wanted to keep him in the loop, in case it turned out his team had used the consultant, and because the investigation could affect our trading operations."

"Later that month, did Otis itself receive a subpoena?"

Malomar took a sip of water and resumed her businesslike, anodyne tone. "Yes, on March twelfth, the company received a grand jury subpoena from the US Attorney's Office. The subpoena said Otis had to produce documents relating to trades placed in 2011 and early 2012 in several of our funds."

Waters introduced the subpoena to Otis. A page appeared on the screen. "Please tell the jury which funds are identified in the subpoena." Malomar read the names of the funds. Then Waters asked: "Do you know whether the defendant, Emma Simpson, managed any of those funds?"

Malomar looked over at Emma and then immediately turned her chestnut brown eyes the other way to avoid eye contact.

Emma pursed her lips. *Keep your poker face*, she thought. *Keep looking at her but don't stare. Remember, you didn't know this at the time, and we will show them that later.*

"Um, yes." Malomar looked at the document and said, "I think she managed the Otis Healthcare Strategies funds—the ones listed as numbers one, two, and three."

Emma glanced at the jury. The Maddow lady and the Democratic Socialist both started scribbling notes. *Keep calm*, Emma reminded herself and focused her attention back to the witness stand.

"Now what, if any, steps did you take after Otis received this subpoena?" Waters asked.

"Several things." Malomar looked up from the document and turned toward the jury. "First, I notified some of our top executives—our General Counsel, who is my boss, as well as Richard Ginsberg, the Chief Executive of the firm, and a few others at our headquarters in Boston, where I work. And we engaged an outside law firm to represent us in this investigation."

"Did you tell anyone in the New York office about the subpoena to Otis?" Waters asked, glancing over at the defense table before turning her gaze back to Malomar. Emma pretended not to notice.

"Yes, I called Doug Jones. He's the one I spoke to earlier about this investigation, as I mentioned."

"Why did you contact Mr. Jones?"

Malomar responded, "Well, some of the documents we had to collect would be in the New York office, so we needed

Doug's help gathering those for the outside lawyers to review and produce."

Emma's jaw dropped. *What?* Her heart was racing. *Doug told me the investigation was about Boston and Delphun. He never told us to collect any documents. Where is this coming from? And anyway, when did this supposedly happen?*

"Now, did there come a time after that conversation with Doug Jones when you sent an email to the entire New York Office about the document retention policy?" Waters asked.

"Yes. I think it was a few days after I spoke to Doug. I heard that people in New York were destroying—"

"Objection, hearsay," Will said coolly. But the veins in his neck were throbbing.

Emma crossed her arms tightly into her chest. Her blood pressure was through the roof. *Even I know that was blatant hearsay. Is Lucy deliberately piling on, or does she not realize how bad this is making me look?*

Waters stood up. "Your Honor, I think I can fix this."

The judge nodded. "The last sentence of the answer is stricken. Jurors, please disregard that." He looked at Waters. "Proceed."

An email dated March 16, 2012, appeared on the small screens only the witness, the judge, and counsel could see. The middle paragraph said: "We have recently learned that in the past several days employees in our New York office have discarded hard copy documents and deleted electronic files in response to emails sent on March 14, 2012, by Ben Noguchi and Emma Simpson about the computer system upgrade, reminding people about the document retention policy."

What the fuck, thought Emma. *How is this "fixing" the problem?*

"Ms. Malomar, is this an email you sent on March 16, 2012, to an email group that included all of Otis's New York employees?"

"Yes."

"Your Honor, we offer this exhibit," Waters said.

Before Waters could even finish her sentence, Will was out of his seat again. "Objection, there are multiple levels of hearsay in the document."

Judge Gregory frowned at Will and said, "Counsel, please come to the sidebar."

White noise started playing from the speakers. Emma bit her lip, watching the lawyers crowd around the sidebar, as she strained in vain to hear what they were saying.

Finally, the lawyers returned to their places. The judge said, "The objection is sustained. Only certain parts of the document will be admitted."

Josh leaned over to Emma and whispered, "He made them redact the hearsay."

Finally, a favorable ruling, thought Emma as she put her pencil down and relaxed her facial muscles.

An email from Malomar to all New York employees appeared on the screen. The subject was "Document Retention Policy Suspended."

The message said:

The document retention policy is being suspended effective *immediately* due to a pending litigation matter.

Please disregard any emails you have received in the past two days instructing you to comply with the firm's document retention policy until further notice.

Lucy A. Malomar
Associate General Counsel

Emma stared wide-eyed at the screen and all the black. *This was supposed to be a good ruling? Now they're going to think we're hiding something.* She glanced at the jurors. Maddow's "boyfriend" was sneering.

Waters asked, "What were you referring to when you said to disregard any emails you have received in the past two days?"

Malomar turned toward the jury. "I was referring to two emails that were sent on March 14, 2012, to all the employees in the New York office. One was sent by Ben Noguchi, and a later one was sent by Emma Simpson responding to Ben's email."

Waters introduced the two emails and then left them on the big screen. "Ms. Malomar, why did you send your own email to the New York Office two days after Emma Simpson and Ben Noguchi sent these emails?"

"Objection," Will said it calmly from his seat but in an authoritative tone.

"Goes to state of mind," said Waters.

"This witness's state of mind is completely irrelevant, judge," Will said drily.

Exactly, thought Emma. *Isn't this trial about my state of mind? Who cares what Malomar thought?* Her heart was beating faster and faster.

"Enough! No speaking objections, counsel. You know better than that," Judge Gregory said with disdain. "I'll allow it."

How can he do that? Why doesn't he just rule without telegraphing his own views? She clenched her fists under the table, afraid to even glance at the jury's reaction.

"Well, we had to make sure no documents that could be called for by the subpoena were destroyed. We were worried that these emails were encouraging people to shred documents we'd need to produce to the government, and that it would look like Otis was hiding evidence."

"Objection!" Will stood up this time but still projected his cool as a cucumber vibe.

The judge looked at the screen with the transcript and furrowed his brow. "Sustained. That last sentence is stricken, and the jury should disregard it."

Emma sighed, feeling utterly defeated. *As if*, she thought, *that's even possible.*

"No further questions." Waters took her notes and left the podium.

Judge Gregory looked up. "All right, ladies and gentlemen, we'll take our lunch break now and return at one thirty."

* * *

Emma was desperate for some fresh air. It was unseasonably nice for November, so she and Pierre took the short walk to Chinatown to grab some takeout. Initially Pierre resisted the idea. "Those paparazzi are probably still out there and will pounce on us and take pictures and shout questions at you. Shouldn't we just go to the cafeteria?"

"I don't give a damn. Let them get their stupid pictures," Emma insisted. "Anyway, I want to try that place with the duck noodle soup all the lawyers rave about." So they went right into the belly of the beast.

Exiting the large Worth Street entrance to the courthouse, Emma and Pierre confronted a wall of men and women lying in wait with video cameras, DSLRs, and boom mikes. They were lined up behind steel railings separating the courthouse from the street—a post 9/11 security measure—like monkeys in cages, shouting and reaching through the bars in hopes of prying snacks out of zoo visitors.

After collecting two steaming containers from New York Noodletown, they sat in the park near the courthouse to eat. The tension that had built up inside ebbed a little as they watched people play pickup basketball and do Tai Chi. The rhythms of the balls hitting the pavement and swooshing through the net and the sleek, slow movements of arms and legs on the figures practicing Tai Chi had a soothing effect on Emma's mood. She closed her eyes and imagined she was gazing at a totally still, turquoise lake that had been formed by an ancient glacier and was encircled by green mountains set against a deep blue sky.

Pierre, on the other hand, seemed distracted. He picked at the noodles with his chopsticks but gave up on the soup after nibbling on a couple of pieces of duck. He set his container aside and turned slightly toward Emma.

"Listen, I've been thinking…" he said slowly. "I should probably get a real job, at least part-time. It's going to take years before the winery turns any profit, and the bills are just going to keep mounting. There'll be college tuition, and we still have a mortgage on the farm."

It was as if a boulder had fallen into Emma's imaginary lake, sending giant waves cascading in every direction. "What do you mean? You think we're going to lose? Is that what you're saying?" she demanded angrily.

"No, no, no. But we have to be more realistic and plan for the worst. Even if you get acquitted, do you really think you'll get your old job back? Do you think it will be easy to find another one?" Pierre crossed his arms. "It's not worth the risk for these companies. They don't care if you're innocent or not. They just care about PR."

"Well, I can keep day trading. Or maybe get hired by a family office, a group that just trades for itself and doesn't have any outside investors," Emma said. *Right? Or was that just pie in the sky?* she wondered. *Am I being delusional?*

"Keep day trading?" Pierre scoffed. He kicked a basketball that had rolled toward the bench they were sitting on, hard, and back toward the players. "What, and piss away more money on fake currencies?"

Emma felt her face smoldering. Her voice got louder. "Don't start on that again," she said angrily. "We've actually made twenty thousand dollars from crypto in just the last several months. And these currencies are no more imaginary than US dollars. They're not paper or gold, but all money is just an intangible that humans have chosen to treat as having value." She frowned. "And anyway, that twenty thousand dollars is more than we've ever made in the five years you've been working on that goddam winery."

"C'mon, Emma. Maybe you're a genius at this, but twenty thousand dollars is a drop in the bucket with the crazy college tuition prices these days. That's not even enough to pay the mortgage or all our other expenses. I'm just trying to be practical here."

Emma put the top on her plastic container of soup, clenched it tightly, stood up, and threw it into the trash can next to their bench. She looked at her watch and said, "We need to get back."

Then she started speed-walking back to the courthouse. Pierre sped after her. She looked back and curled her lip as he darted to catch up.

"Anyway, what would you do? You haven't practiced law in years."

* * *

They made it back on time but just barely. Emma resumed her position in the courtroom as the judge was taking the bench and calling for the jury to be brought in. Malomar was back on the stand, pushing a stray hair back to its rightful place in her perfect coif while she glanced at the clock in the back of the courtroom.

Judge Gregory peered down. "Cross-examination?"

"Thank you, Judge," Will said as he buttoned his sleek forest green suit jacket, strode to the podium, adjusted his glasses, and opened his thin black binder. "Good afternoon, Ms. Malomar."

"Good afternoon."

"Ms. Malomar, you've been practicing law for only a few years, correct?"

"Well, it's actually eight years," Malomar replied. "So a little more than a few."

Will smiled. "Fair enough. And you've been at Otis just two years, right?"

"That's right," Malomar said.

"And before that, you were an associate at the Sullivan & Jones law firm, right?"

"Yes," Malomar said tentatively. "That's true."

"When you worked there, you became an expert on securities regulations, correct?"

Malomar pursed her lips. "Well, I don't know that I'm an expert, exactly. But I'm pretty familiar with SEC regulations for hedge funds, private equity, investment advisers, the rules about insider trading, and so on."

"And that's why you got the job at Otis Capital, right?"

"Yes, I suppose so." Malomar nodded primly. "They were looking for someone with a regulatory background for my position."

"When you were at Sullivan and Jones, you never did any litigation, right?"

"Uh, no." Malomar straightened her headband. *She seems just a tad nervous,* thought Emma. *As if unsure where this is going. Good, hopefully she won't get too far out over her skis.*

"In fact, the only litigation you've ever worked on was an employment dispute at Otis, right?"

"Right, and we used an outside law firm to handle that."

"You relied on outside lawyers for litigation because that wasn't your area, right?" Will asked.

"Right." Malomar responded.

"And you never represented any clients under investigation while you were at Sullivan & Jones, right?"

"No," Malomar said.

"Never had to deal with a government investigation before this one, right?"

"Right."

"And by the way, as far as you know, at the time of this incident, Ms. Simpson also had never dealt with any investigation, right?"

"Objection," interjected Waters immediately.

Judge Gregory removed his reading glasses and peered down at Malomar. "If you know, you may answer."

Malomar took the cue. "I don't know." *Ugh, really? As if she wouldn't have known if I had ever before been the subject of an investigation? She knows better.* Emma clenched her teeth.

"And in fact, your boss, the General Counsel, was not a litigator either, was he?" Will continued.

"No, he was a very experienced corporate lawyer," Malomar explained. "Our practice was to consult external counsel as necessary for litigation or investigation issues."

"Now," Will said, "when you learned that Otis's Boston consultant got a subpoena, you didn't direct anyone at Otis to preserve any documents, did you?"

"No," said Malomar.

"It never occurred to you that that was necessary, did it?"

"Objection!" Waters said loudly.

"Sustained." Judge Gregory smirked as he said it.

"And to this day, as far as you know, there is no legal obligation to preserve documents just because *another company* got a subpoena about something you worked on with them, right?"

"Objection." Waters stood up and shook her head.

"Counsel, you know better." The judge admonished Will. "Sustained." *Great, way to let the jury know you think my lawyer is sleazy.* Emma gripped the table tightly and then took a deep breath.

"Let's discuss the subpoena to Otis," Will continued, unfazed. "One common way to ensure that documents are preserved if you do get a subpoena is to send what's known as a document hold notice, right?"

"Sure," Malomar said.

"And that's a notice sent to employees who might have responsive documents, right?" Will asked.

"Yes."

"And the notice typically gives background about the subpoena and instructs people to retain specific categories of documents, right?"

Malomar agreed.

"And another obvious way to make sure that people who may have responsive documents retain them is to show them the subpoena, right?" Will continued.

Malomar narrowed her eyes. "Well, you could do that, but—"

"But you didn't do that here. Did you?" Will's voice was slow and mellifluous, with just a touch of emphasis on "here."

"Well, I sent the subpoena to our outside counsel, and we were awaiting their guidance as to what to do next. I did show it to the GC and some other top executives, of course," Malomar said, more hesitantly.

Right, some *top executives—but not the ones in New York.*

"But you never sent *Ms. Simpson* a copy of the subpoena, did you?" Will asked coolly.

"No, as I said, we were waiting for advice from outside counsel as to next steps. And I told Emma's compliance officer, Doug Jones, about the subpoena, as we've discussed," Malomar insisted. *She's getting pretty defensive. Is that really what we want?* Emma wondered. She noticed that the fish on Malomar's scarf were upside-down, as if floating dead on top of the water.

"But you didn't do that until several days after you received the subpoena, right?"

Malomar paused and shot a quick glance at Emma for the first time. Then she said, "That's true. I don't remember exactly when I told him. It was soon after we got the subpoena but not right away."

"So it could have been *after* March fourteenth. Isn't that right?" Will kept his eyes trained, laser-like, on her.

There was a long pause. Emma held her breath. Then Malomar said softly, "Yes, that's possible," and looked down at her scarf. She turned it around, and the fish were revived and facing right-side up again.

Will waited for Malomar to look at him again. Then he said, "And you didn't *send* the subpoena to Doug Jones until *after* Ms. Simpson and Mr. Noguchi sent their March fourteenth emails, right?"

Malomar smoothed out her scarf, gripping it tightly. "I believe that is correct, yes."

"And when you spoke on the phone, before you sent the subpoena," Will said, "you didn't read Mr. Jones the list of thirty categories of documents the subpoena requested, did you?"

"No," Malomar agreed.

The page of the subpoena listing the funds appeared on the screen. "Did you inform Mr. Jones that the government had demanded documents relating to Otis Healthcare Strategies one?"

"Not specifically, no," Malomar conceded.

"You didn't tell him the government had asked the company to produce documents about Otis Healthcare Strategies two either. did you?"

"Not specifically, no," Malomar said.

"Not generally either, right?" Will continued.

"No."

"And what about Otis Healthcare Strategies three? You didn't tell Mr. Jones that was in the subpoena either, did you?"

"No." Malomar started twirling a small strand of hair and then looked up.

Will said, "Let's get page five of the subpoena on the screen. Now, ma'am, do you see this list of trades by Otis?"

"Yes."

"When you first spoke to Mr. Jones about the subpoena, you didn't read this list of fifty trades to him, did you?"

"No," Malomar said, tugging at her scarf again. *She's getting a little rattled, but does that help? Don't we want her to explain why she wasn't rushing to tell us to preserve all the documents?*

"Ms. Malomar, isn't it a fact that the only specific trades on this list you mentioned to Mr. Jones during that call were the Delphun trades?" Will fixed his eyes intently on Malomar.

"Yes, I definitely did mention Delphun and my concerns about Delphun. There may have been others too, but I don't recall all the specifics. My objective was just to let him know we'd gotten a subpoena and give him a heads up since his team might have documents," Malomar said. "And as I said, we were waiting for guidance from the outside law firm about what to collect. They were the experts. I'm sure I mentioned the law firm, since they would probably need to speak to him."

Will leaned forward and relaxed his facial muscles as he looked at Malomar. "They were the experts, and you needed their guidance because you and your boss didn't have experience with investigations, right?"

Malomar let go of her scarf and put her hand back in her lap as she looked up, relieved to be off the hook. "Right, as I said earlier, I'm more of a regulatory person, and my boss is a corporate lawyer. That's why we hired a former US Attorney to handle our response to this subpoena."

"And that's why, when you spoke to Mr. Jones, you didn't tell him to instruct the employees in New York that the document retention policy was suspended, right?"

"Correct."

Will gripped the podium tightly and paused. "Now, ma'am, isn't it a fact that you didn't do that because you didn't know that was necessary?"

Waters jumped up. "Objection, Your Honor."

Judge Gregory looked at Waters and then at the screen with the transcript, which he perused for a moment. "Sustained."

"And if you had known that was required, *of course* you would have instructed Mr. Jones to immediately direct employees in his office to preserve documents called for by the subpoena. Will paused. "Isn't that right?"

"Objection." Waters was on her feet again.

"Sustained."

Emma sighed. *Is the judge going to even listen to the cross and think about it before ruling?* she wondered. *Or is he too busy googling his press coverage for this case?*

"Your Honor, can we have a sidebar?" Will inquired.

The judge groaned and then glanced at the clock. "We have to break early today because I have a speech to give, so you're a lucky man, Mr. Shelby. Why don't we discuss it after I excuse the jury?"

He looked at the jurors and smiled. "Thank you for your attention, ladies and gentlemen, and have a nice evening. We'll resume tomorrow at nine thirty, okay?" He nodded to Malomar. "You may step down, ma'am."

Everyone stood up, the jurors filed out, and Malomar left the courtroom.

Will took a deep breath. He trained his eyes on the judge. "Your Honor, it appears the government will object to this entire line of questions, which is critical to the defense. What we are trying to show is that even the lawyers at Otis didn't think they had any obligation to preserve documents after they learned about the Delphun investigation." He paused. "We have evidence showing Ms. Malomar spoke to the General Counsel and the CEO as well as the portfolio managers who traded Delphun about the investigation. The in-house lawyers did gather information. They asked questions about the trades and the relationship with the consultant. But they didn't warn anyone not to delete relevant documents. That never crossed their mind—probably because they hadn't dealt with this type of situation before. And even after they got a subpoena, they waited for advice from outside counsel before issuing guidance. Obviously, they believed that was appropriate."

Waters remained standing during Will's entire speech and was chomping at the bit. As soon as he paused, she started talking in a rapid-fire mode as the court reporter struggled to keep up.

Waters said, "Judge, none of that is *remotely* relevant to the issues in this case. The issue is Ms. Simpson's state of mind. The thoughts and discussions of others at the company about the subpoenas and investigation have nothing to do with what was in *her* head. We're not here for a mini-trial about what these other people talked about and what they should or shouldn't have done. Ms. Simpson is the one on trial here."

Will was still standing too. He jumped back into the fray. "This evidence is clearly admissible, and it *is* relevant to what Ms. Simpson's state of mind was and whether she thought she was doing anything wrong, Your Honor. The point here is that Otis's lawyers obviously didn't think there was any need to make sure everyone preserved documents just because *another company* got a subpoena, so how would Ms. Simpson have known that? They also didn't rush to send a preservation notice even after Otis got a subpoena. They're not litigators. They didn't know what to do, so they waited for guidance from external counsel. Ms. Simpson wasn't even a lawyer, and she knew far less about any of this. So how would she have known there was anything wrong with sending her email? This is important support for her defense."

Will cleared his throat.

The judge pursed his lips. "Mr. Shelby, I do think the government has a point, but I want to mull this over some more. Both sides should file letter briefs on this by nine o'clock this evening. And please submit any documents the defense proposes to introduce on these topics. You'll have my ruling tomorrow morning by nine o'clock."

"Absolutely, Judge," Will responded. "Thank you."

CHAPTER 13

PROSECUTION'S CASE (II)

NOVEMBER 6, 2014

TRIBECA, NEW YORK, NEW YORK

The blaring screech of the alarm buzzer shot through the silence, blasting Emma out of her fitful slumber.

Don't think. Just do it, or there won't be time, she said to herself as she pulled on her running clothes.

She skipped out of her room, down the stairs, and out of the hotel's front door, pounding through the bustling city streets and dodging the traffic on her way to the running path near the Hudson River. As her feet hit the pavement, one-two, one-two, one-two, the wind whipped through her hair and numbed her fingers through the thin black neoprene gloves. She pulled her thumbs and fingers out of their sheaths, leaving them dangling as she made fists in the gloves to generate warmth, and picked up her pace.

She ran uptown, passing a high school, playgrounds, Chelsea Piers and its urban golf course, a heliport, and the giant Intrepid Museum ship. These structures shielded the banal suburban New Jersey landscape beyond the river, which still popped into view every so often. To her right, cars and trucks and buses zipped along, occasionally honking or stopping at traffic lights. The path itself was filled with joggers, rollerbladers, and people walking dogs. Emma also had to dodge the occasional bicycle that whizzed by. All of this pandemonium was somehow comforting. It provided a rhythmic backdrop to her gait and a smorgasbord of sights and sounds to divert her thoughts away from the drama unfolding in Foley Square.

By the time she arrived back in her hotel room after her six-mile run, Emma's face was glowing a healthy pink. She was drenched with sweat and had removed the gloves altogether. She was still thinking about that weird-looking IAC building and how those oddly shaped walls—however interesting architecturally—could possibly house practical office spaces.

It was 8:00 a.m. Emma grabbed her phone and glanced at the lock screen's image of Daniel and Sarah from last year's holiday card. *They look so happy*, she thought. What a difference a year makes. She'd spoken to them last night after dinner but wanted to see their faces, even if just for a few minutes before they ran off to school. She tapped the Facetime app.

She heard the low throttle of the *dring, dring, dring* sound three times and then saw the pale cyan paint of her kitchen ceiling on the screen and Sarah's disembodied voice. "Hi, Mom!" The picture moved away from the ceiling and down until it displayed a view of her daughter sitting behind a plate of half-eaten eggs and a glass of orange juice.

Emma smiled warmly and her eyes sparkled. "Hey, baby girl. Just wanted to say hi quickly before you guys head to school. I miss you."

"I miss you too. I can't really talk—gotta pack my stuff for school. But good luck today! Love you." Sarah blew her a kiss and handed the phone to Daniel.

"Wait, Sarah—make sure to put on a sweater," Emma said. "It's really cold here today, so it must be even colder there."

But Sarah had scooted off, and Daniel appeared on camera. He ran his hand through his hair and looked at her.

"Hi, Daniel," Emma said.

Daniel rested the phone on something so it would stay vertical as he poured some powder and water into a Nalgene bottle, closed the lid, and shook it up. His mouth was closed and his lips pursed together, as if his teeth were clenched. He said nothing for what seemed an eternity. But at least he didn't hang up the phone.

Then he looked into the camera and said, "Were you running? Seems like that would be hard, with all the cars. Don't you have to stop all the time at traffic lights?"

Emma laughed. "I know what you mean, but the hotel's pretty close to a path on the river with no cars, so I went there. It wasn't bad—kind of interesting sights but too many people."

"Cool," Daniel said, grabbing an apple. "Sounds like that lawyer didn't hurt your case too much yesterday. I hope today goes well too." He held up two crossed fingers. The corners of his mouth turned upward just a tiny bit, and then he said, "Gotta go, Mom," and hung up.

Well, at least he wasn't as sullen this morning. *Maybe tonight I can even have a conversation with him,* Emma thought hopefully as she reached down to pick up the *Wall Street Journal* that was slid under her door. *Maybe if I get acquitted, he will be more like his old self—especially since he finally put that Snapchat drama behind him and made varsity basketball.*

But suddenly reality clobbered her over the head. The headline below the fold on the front page said, "Lawyer Testifies Against Disgraced Hedge Fund Manager." Emma couldn't bear to read the article. The press about the case was always negative, no matter what happened. She threw the newspaper against the wall in disgust and collapsed to the floor, her head in her hands. She sat like that for a minute or two.

Then she headed for the shower—though the run was already completely washed off—and braced for her return to battle. It was time to get her pads, suit up, and head to the arena for the next round.

* * *

500 PEARL STREET, NEW YORK, NEW YORK

And that next round started with a pummeling—a shot straight to the head.

The judge got right to business at 9:00 a.m. sharp, just moments after Emma and the lawyers arrived in the courtroom.

"Please be seated." He scowled in her general direction and then snarled straight at Will before announcing in his nasal voice, "All right, counsel, I've read your submissions, and I'm going to sustain the government's objections. There will be no cross-examination about the Otis lawyers' internal discussions and deliberations or their beliefs about what obligations they had to preserve documents when they first learned about the investigation, or after they got the subpoena. That has no bearing on whether Ms. Simpson knew she was doing something wrong when she sent her email urging her colleagues to destroy documents on March fourteenth. And all of the proffered defense exhibits on these topics are excluded."

Emma felt all the blood rushing to her brain. *What the fuck? How could he keep this out? And what was that about urging her colleagues to destroy documents? That's how he describes my email? Talk about putting a thumb on the scales. This was a lead weight.*

His Honor was still talking. "This is simply irrelevant, a side-show that will distract and confuse the jury. The discussions of other people at Otis about this are neither here nor there. The issue here is whether *this defendant* obstructed justice." He wouldn't even use her name.

A wave of nausea started burbling up from Emma's stomach.

Will stood up and started to open his mouth, but the judge banged his gavel loudly and said, "That's my ruling. We'll resume with the jury at nine thirty." Then he disappeared into the robing room.

When the jury arrived, Malomar resumed the stand, but with the cross disemboweled, not much was left to do. Will did get her to admit the investigators seemed most interested in Delphun and some consultant Boston was using. He also got Malomar to take the jury through some of Emma's contributions to building Otis, fueling its growth, and even her support for strong ethics and compliance training. The testimony wasn't a total and complete disaster, but it sure ended with a whimper.

After Malomar stepped down—still looking away as if afraid even to acknowledge Emma's existence—Ted Hardin rose to his feet and announced: "The government calls Mikhail Kuznetsov."

Mikey, as Emma knew him, emerged from the back of the courtroom and slowly made his way to the stand, flicking his mousy-brown cowlick out of his eyes as he shuffled across the heavy carpet. She remembered interviewing him. He must have been about twenty-one then—shy, not an arrogant bone in the kid's body, but light years smarter than just about anyone she'd ever met before. Now, he faced straight ahead but shifted his eyes slightly and caught hers without moving his head as he walked by the defense table.

A sliver of a sheepish half-smile fleetingly crossed his face. It happened in a flash.

He's not trying to hurt me, she thought. *It's not his fault they dragged him into this. And at least his lawyer agreed to speak to Will about his testimony.* Her blood rushed to her head just thinking about that sniveling little jerk.

"Mr. Kuznetsov, what do you do for a living?" Hardin inquired.

"I'm research analyst for Otis Capital, focusing on health care stocks." Mikey still dropped articles from time to time when he spoke, though his Russian accent was barely perceptible.

"What are your responsibilities in that position?"

"To conduct research into public companies in the health care industry and make recommendations for investments for our hedge fund managers," Mikey replied.

"How long have you worked at Otis?"

"Five years," Mikey said.

"Was that your first job?" Hardin asked.

"It was my first job after college. I worked as waiter while studying at MIT," Mikey said.

"Do you know the defendant, Emma Simpson?"

"Yes, I do," Mikey said softly.

"How long have you known her?"

"Around five years. I met her when I interviewed to work for Otis." Mikey took a sip of water.

"Did you work with Ms. Simpson when she was at Otis?" Hardin asked.

"Sometimes. She wasn't my direct supervisor for long since she was promoted to run office a year or two after I started. But she encouraged all analysts to share their ideas with her, and she was pretty hands-on and liked to brainstorm with us. She'd read our reports carefully and then grill us with questions, send us to get more data, stuff like that." Mikey got more animated as he went along.

"Did you view her as a mentor of sorts?"

"Yes, definitely. She was really good boss, very supportive," Mikey said enthusiastically, looking at the jury. The hardware store guy was nodding.

Emma tried to conceal a smile at first but then shifted gears. *Why is Hardin eliciting this? He must know that Mikey will say good things about me. Where's this going?* She started rubbing her hands through her hair.

Hardin looked at Mikey, pressed his hands into the sides of the podium, and seemed to grow taller as he straightened his back. "Mr. Kuznetsov, are you testifying voluntarily here today?"

Mikey looked over at the judge and then back at Hardin. "I'm not sure what you mean."

"Are you testifying because the government issued a subpoena compelling you to come to court?"

"Oh, yes, there was subpoena. Right." Mikey looked at Emma.

She started tapping her pen against her skirt at a staccato beat.

"Now, Mr. Kuznetsov, I'd like to direct your attention to March 14, 2012. Did you attend a staff meeting in Otis's New York office that day?"

"Yes."

"Who else was present?" Hardin asked, looking down at his notes.

Mikey paused. "Ms. Simpson, Ben Noguchi, Doug Jones—he's in legal and compliance—and couple of other analysts—Dylan Morrison, probably Olivia Snow, I think, but I'm not sure. That may have been the week she was out sick with flu."

"What topics were discussed at the meeting?" Hardin asked.

Mikey rested his chin on his hand and then put it down and leaned into the microphone. "Um, the normal subjects for these meetings—how funds were doing, intel we had about companies we were invested in or were following for possible investment, things like that."

"Did the topic of PLP come up?" Hardin queried.

"Objection, leading," Will said from his seat.

"Overruled." Mikey said nothing. The judge looked at him. "You may answer."

Mikey nodded. "Yes, I don't remember exactly what was said, but someone mentioned PLP and the possibility of hiring consultants who worked with them, who might help us research some pharmaceutical products under development by companies we were researching."

"And what is PLP?"

"PLP is name of, like, what we call expert network firm. They connect consultants who are experts in different industries with clients looking for consultants to advise them in these areas. We sometimes used these firms in our securities research." Mikey looked at the jury. "It's common in investment business to use these kinds of firms; pretty typical."

Hardin narrowed his eyes and tapped his fingers on the podium.

Guess he didn't like that little comment, thought Emma. *Not in the script, apparently.* She pressed her lips together to suppress a smile.

"What happened after someone mentioned PLP?" Hardin asked.

"Doug said we should make sure to diligence these consultants before retaining any of them. He said there were government investigations about whether some shady consultants were giving inside information. I think they were at some other firm, not PLP, but anyway he wanted us to be super cautious about this." Mikey stopped. He looked at Ted.

"Did he say anything else?" Hardin prompted.

"Um, I think he mentioned something about subpoena. Like, there was subpoena, not about PLP specifically or anything, but he said something about investigation into Otis trading." Mikey looked down, trying to avert his gaze from Emma for the first time.

"Did he mention which trades were being investigated?" Hardin asked.

"I don't think so; I don't remember that."

"Did he say what Otis office the subpoena concerned?"

"No," Mikey said. "I don't remember that."

Emma's pulse rate quickened, and she squeezed her fists together tightly. It didn't happen the way he said, but she knew that meeting was why they called him. To muddy the waters on the details. It still felt like a kick in the ass, though.

Now Hardin leaned into the podium. "Were you surprised to learn about the subpoena?"

Will shot up. "Objection."

"Goes to state of mind, Judge," Hardin rejoined.

"His state of mind is irrelevant, Your Honor," Will said coolly.

The judge, who had been looking at the computer screen that did not have the transcript, must have been reading something that lightened his mood. Or maybe he forgot who had objected. He looked up and said, "Sustained."

Hardin narrowed his eyes slightly but looked at his notes and moved on. "Did there come a time, later in the day on March 14, 2012, when you received an email about the Otis document retention policy?"

"Yeah, I got two emails—one from Ben, reminding us to follow policy, and then later that night, another one from Emma—Ms. Simpson—sort of seconding Ben's advice," Mikey said matter-of-factly.

Hardin showed him the two emails and had him read them to the jury. Then he asked, "What, if anything, did you do after receiving these emails?"

Emma gritted her teeth and looked down at the table. These next few minutes were going to feel as if her nails were slowly being pulled out of her fingers. *Ugh, now we're going to hear about all the document destruction,* she thought.

Mikey looked sheepish. "Well, I'm a bit of a pack rat, frankly, and when I saw these emails, I figured I better clean out my desk as soon as possible. I take lots of notes when I'm doing research—notes of calls, notes of what I'm reading, things like that—but we're not supposed to keep that stuff after we write up our research memos. So the next day when I got to office, I went through my files and threw out all my notes from old reports and deleted other stuff we're not supposed to retain from my computer."

"Did you delete emails?" Ted asked.

"Yeah, files on computer, and I double deleted emails out of Outlook trash folder," Mikey said. The transit worker shook his head a few times and jotted down a note.

Hardin leaned forward into the podium. "Do you know if anyone else destroyed any documents after Ms. Simpson sent her March fourteenth email about the document policy?"

Mikey paused. "Yes, a lot of us work in open bullpen, so you can see what other analysts and staffers are doing. I saw other people cleaning out their desks the next day too. It was very noisy, like flurry of activity. The shredding bins got pretty full by end of second day."

The Democratic Socialist juror was taking copious notes. The Maddow girl turned toward her "boyfriend" and raised her eyebrows. First Malomar, now this. It was far worse than having her fingernails pulled out, Emma thought; it was like she was being waterboarded or having all the air sucked out of her lungs by a vacuum cleaner. Would she ever breathe again?

"No further questions," Hardin announced.

Judge Gregory banged his gavel. "We'll take our lunch break. Please be back by one thirty," he said as the jury left the courtroom, whispering to each other in hushed tones. Then he walked off the bench.

Emma felt dizzy and faint. She bolted out of the courtroom and dashed to the ladies' room. She locked herself in the first stall she could get to, leaned over the toilet, and threw up.

CHAPTER 14

PROSECUTION'S CASE (III)

NOVEMBER 7, 2014

ONE SAINT ANDREW'S PLAZA, NEW YORK, NEW YORK

It was 5:00 p.m., and Annie Waters had finally gotten back to her desk after a long day—in fact, a long week—of trial. She was getting organized before her Saturday meeting to prep the government's next witness—one of the Otis lawyers who had interviewed Emma Simpson early in the investigation. Annie pulled up her draft Q&A and the lawyer's memo of the interview and started going through them to make sure she was covering the key points—the statements the prosecution team thought were false. This would be important, especially if Emma Simpson took the stand and changed her story.

The phone rang. She glanced at the caller ID. It was the FBI case agent, Bill Marsh. Annie swiped right and tapped the speaker icon on her phone. "Hey, Bill. What's up?"

"Annie, you're not going to believe this, but I just found something that may be huge. I don't know if you guys have seen it, but it looks like notes from a staff meeting from the day Simpson sent the email, and it mentions our subpoena! How can Simpson say she wasn't trying to get people to destroy evidence if she knew about the subpoena *before* she sent that email?"

Annie's jaw dropped. Her mind raced through a million questions and contradictory emotions. This could be devastating. It could seal the case and blow the lid off the defense. But why hadn't they known about this before? The team had been through the databases so many times, and they'd had all this material for nearly two years *before* filing the indictment. How could they turn it over now, right before resting their case, without causing a mistrial? The defense would raise a huge stink. The judge would go nuts.

"Bill, you have *got* to be kidding! What the eff? How are you just finding this now? Where was it? Send it to me ASAP. I need to talk to Ted so we can figure out what to do."

Bill responded, "Sending it now. I found a hard copy printout in a folder with a bunch of other documents I was pulling together for one of the charts you guys asked us to make."

Annie said, "All right, let me take a look and we'll call you back."

She opened Bill's email and quickly scanned the attached PDF. It was two pages of handwritten notes with what appeared to be the date "3/14" at the top. The handwriting was pretty cryptic. Some of the notes seemed to relate to several companies Simpson's team had positions in and what appeared to be "to do" research items. At the bottom of the second page was this:

DJ—Doug Jones, the in-house Otis lawyer in the New York office? It sure looked like a reference to something Jones had said about a subpoena to Otis. But the reference to "Delphun" was ambiguous. The grand jury subpoena did relate in part to Delphun, but the Delphun aspect of the investigation was related to Otis's Boston office and wasn't about the New York group.

And Simpson claimed that she thought the investigation related to trading by the Boston office and had nothing to do with New York. Wasn't this at least arguably exculpatory? It seemed to support her defense, after all.

On the other hand, Simpson told Otis's lawyers during the internal investigation that she didn't remember hearing about the subpoena until *after* she sent the email, so this helped put the lie to that story.

But at best, the notes were a mixed bag. Plus, there were two big potential downsides here: one, this might *help* the defense; and two, there would probably be a veritable shit-storm because Annie didn't think the document had ever been turned over in discovery.

Annie grabbed her laptop and ran into Ted's office, practically yelling. "Ted, you have got to see this! Bill just sent me something wild. I'm pretty sure I didn't know we had this." She walked over to his side of the desk and showed him her screen.

Ted's eyes lit up. He was wearing a tight, midnight blue T-shirt that made them look like shiny sapphires and revealed his tight, well-defined arm muscles and six-pack abs. "Holy shit! This is dynamite," he said. "It will blow up the defense. How can Simpson say she didn't hear about the subpoena before she emailed everyone to destroy documents? Where did this come from? Why wasn't it on our exhibit list before?"

He flashed one of those disarming smiles that could suck you in like a vacuum cleaner as he rubbed his hands together, grinning.

"Wait 'til the jury sees *this*! We should introduce it tomorrow during the testimony about Simpson's false statements to the internal investigators. Elicit her lie about not knowing about any subpoena until *after* she sent the email, and then introduce these notes—"

Wasn't Ted getting ahead of himself again? He was like a poster child for confirmation bias. Every new piece of information was more evidence to support his theory about what happened. He had been like this from the beginning of this case, early in the investigation, and he was doing it again now.

On the other hand, she thought, *maybe I'm being too cautious. I guess now that we're in trial, we do have to find a way to take advantage of this. But we still need to deal with the fallout.*

"Ted, not so fast," she tried to focus him on the problems this new information created. "First of all, it says 'Boston,' and 'Delphun' is circled, and that's..."

Ted cut her off. "So what? It doesn't say the subpoena was *only* about Delphun, and we know from Frances O'Brien that people at Otis knew we were looking at other trades, including ones the New York group was doing."

"But, Ted," Annie groaned, "this could be Brady. Or at least that's what Simpson's lawyers will say. They'll say we should have disclosed it ages ago. And have we turned it over? I'm not sure we have, since I, for one, have never seen it before—and it sure sounds like you haven't either. We've got to mark it and get it out to the defense, stat. But they're going to go ballistic."

Ted scoffed. "We can deal with that. Let's wait until tomorrow. Just bury it in some other documents."

Annie twisted her lips together. "I guess that's fine too. Maybe some of the compliance manuals and some of the other exhibits we're putting in on Monday?"

Ted said, "Sure, sounds good. I wouldn't worry about it, though. There's no way Judge Gregory keeps it out, even if it turns out it wasn't in any of the productions. It's too critical."

Was this really the right thing to do? Annie thought anxiously. Would they really get away with burying the document in a bunch of compliance manuals? Maybe they should run it by one of the Unit Chiefs to get some cover at least. "Ted, should we see what Jared thinks?"

Ted rolled his eyes. "Oh, come on. This was probably in the discovery, anyway. And we have to use it. Plus, you know how difficult he can be to reach on Friday nights. Let it go. I need to focus on the summation—and I need to add this to my PowerPoint. This is awesome."

Annie paused and then said, "Okay, I guess you're right."

She returned to her office, resigned. Was something wrong with her? Was this the right job for her? Why could she not get excited about this like Ted? Why was she always filled with trepidation whenever there was an unexpected development? She sighed and started looking through her Outlook folders for the case, searching for the "production letters" they had sent to the defense, to try to figure out if these notes had been produced. It didn't look that way, but it would be a tedious task to know for sure.

Annie asked the paralegal to mark the notes as an exhibit and add it to the list for Monday. Then she pulled up an email she had previously drafted for the defense lawyers, which covered several items related to the next trial day—which witnesses they anticipated calling and a note about an additional summary chart they expected to provide later in the weekend.

She added at the bottom: "In addition, we've attached the following documents," with a list of fourteen exhibit numbers. She described the notes as "GX373—we intend to offer this on Monday. Let us know if you will stipulate to authenticity."

Annie saved the email in her drafts folder and resumed work on her Q&A of the lawyer who was going to testify about Emma's false statements to Otis's outside counsel.

* * *

NOVEMBER 9, 2014

885 THIRD AVENUE, NEW YORK, NEW YORK

Snow was lightly falling in dry, small flakes as Will emerged from the E train. His red and white Stan Smith shoes made slight imprints on the white dust coating the pavement, melting it briefly as he entered the Lipstick building. It was hard to tell whether it would stick or not. Hopefully Nia would be able to take the boys sledding in Riverside Park today, even if he was going to be stuck here all day prepping Emma and working on his closing.

Just as well, he thought. *I'm too exhausted for sledding anyway.*

He entered the elevator and glanced at his phone. Good, there was the revised draft of Emma's direct with the changes he'd asked Josh to make. He saw a few other messages from the trial team and an email from Annie Waters about tomorrow's witnesses, a summary chart, and a bunch of exhibits. The usual stuff. The doors opened, and he headed over to his office.

The desk phone was ringing as he walked in; the caller ID flashed Josh's office number. It stopped ringing before he reached his desk. Shrugging, he took his jacket off and hung it on the door. As he was about to leave his office to grab coffee, Pink Floyd's "Fearless" started playing in his pocket. He took out his phone; there was Josh's caller ID again. He sighed and answered the call. "What's up? I just got in," he said sharply.

"Have you seen that email from Waters?" Josh asked breathlessly.

"I saw there was an email about the witness list and some exhibits, but I haven't had a chance to study it yet. As I said,

I just got here. I was literally taking off my coat when you called." Will still had an edge in his voice.

"Sorry, but this is unbelievable. You're going to have a cow when you see it. One of the exhibits is a document I'm sure we've never seen before—and it's dynamite! It will blow up their whole case." Josh was talking a mile a minute.

"What is the document? Get to the point," Will said as he sat down and waited impatiently for his computer to start up.

"It's notes dated March 14, 2012—apparently from the morning staff meeting when Jones told them about the subpoena—and the notes say 'DJ: Boston-Subpoena,' and then the word 'Delphun,' which is *circled*," Josh said. "It's the attachment marked GX373 if you've got the email up on your screen. Look at the bottom of the second page."

Will opened the document, scrolled down to the bottom, and saw the notes. His eyes popped out of his head. "Holy shit! How could they not have turned this over before? This proves our entire defense."

He looked at the cover email again. It was *long*. He scanned it, looking for any discussion of the new document while Josh said, "I know. And they don't even admit it's a new document or acknowledge that it's Brady. She just includes it together with a list of other things we've seen before and says what the exhibit numbers will be. It's like either they don't realize it wasn't disclosed, or they're trying to hide it."

"Oh, believe me, they know we've never seen this before. Are you fucking kidding me?" Will felt his blood pressure going through the roof. "We are going to raise holy hell about this. Come to my office. *Now.*"

He started pacing and glanced out the window while waiting for Josh to arrive. The snow was falling faster and more densely. The void between the white dots was filling in quickly as they disintegrated into a white blur. *How could this be happening at this stage?* he thought. *If we had those notes earlier, we could have opened on them, we could have shown them to Kuznetsov. Who knows, maybe we could even have persuaded Weisman to drop the case.*

Josh burst in, out of breath. Will waved at him to sit down. "Obviously, we should double-check to be absolutely sure we didn't already have it, but assuming we're certain about that, we've got to move for a mistrial. This is a blatant Brady violation. They've had this for months, they try to disguise its importance now, and the government is about to rest. It's too late for us to be able to meaningfully use it. Write a letter that we can send the judge today. Get me a draft ASAP."

"What about Emma?" Josh asked.

"What do you mean?" *Millennials,* Will thought. *Can't deal with pressure or learn to walk and chew gum at the same time. How's this kid going to handle first-chairing a trial?* "Don't worry about it. Michiko and I will meet with her while you write the letter," he said as he ushered Josh out of the office and headed down the hall to get his coffee at last.

* * *

An hour later, he was showing Emma a printout of the notes in the conference room with Michiko, the junior associate. Emma's eyes were sparkling with delight. "I told you!" she said, slamming her hand on the table. "Doug said this was about Boston and the Delphun trades. And these notes confirm it." She looked at him, eager for vindication. "This is going to help us a lot isn't it?"

"Well, I hope so, but it would have been a lot better if we could have used it earlier. Maybe if we had showed them to

Mikey, he would have refined his testimony about what he heard about the investigation, or at least dialed it back a bit." Will sighed. He didn't want to crush her enthusiasm but was worried about her expectations being too high. "And I can't believe they are really planning to introduce this themselves, so we have to be sure we can get these notes into evidence," he said.

"Wait, why would the government want to introduce this?" Emma asked.

"I'm not sure—maybe to take the sting out, defuse it? Maybe they will say it confirms that you knew about the subpoena, and that's all that really matters?" Will stroked his chin. "Do you know who wrote them? Do you recognize this handwriting?"

"It looks like Ben's handwriting to me," said Emma.

Will's eyes narrowed. *Shit*, he thought, *just about the worst possible answer; we can't call him. He'll take the Fifth since he hasn't been sentenced yet.* "Well, let's see if we can get them in through Doug if the government doesn't introduce them."

He grabbed a couple of water bottles and handed her one.

"Anyway, let's go through your testimony again. I want to spend a couple of hours on the direct, and then my partner, Andy Bernstein, will do some mock cross."

* * *

Will sauntered back to his desk four hours later, thinking the prep session went pretty well. Emma was the rare client who would probably help herself by testifying—if she could control herself. Of course, who knew what she would actually do under the pressure, especially if that prick Hardin did the cross. If he could light the right spark, she might explode and blow up the case. But still, if the jury believed her, she would be home free.

He opened the outline of his summation and started sketching out more details when the "Fearless" song rang out again. Doug Jones's lawyer's name flashed across his phone. He tapped the answer icon and said, "Will Shelby here."

"Hey, buddy, it's Cris." She sounded chagrined. "Listen, I'm really sorry about this—we had no choice really—but I have bad news."

Will's heart sank. He knew what she was going to say. What else could it be? His voice was filled with trepidation. "What do you mean? Is this about Doug?" Dumb question. It wasn't as if they had any other matters to be discussing on a Sunday in the middle of Emma's trial.

"Yes," she said dully. "He can't testify. They told me if he does, and he says he told her there was an investigation of a Boston consultant about Delphun trades, they'll go after him for perjury. He's taking the Fifth. I'm sorry."

"But, Cris, they just produced some notes that corroborate his account. Notes about Boston and Delphun," Will said.

"I wasn't aware of those notes. Were they Doug's?" Cris asked.

"No, we think they're Ben's," Will said. "But I can send them to you so you can ask him."

"Anyway, it doesn't really change anything," Cris said sheepishly. "They also said he had exposure for obstruction since he saw Ben's first email but didn't stop Ben from sending a similar one to whole the New York team. He's got no choice. He really can't testify."

Will stood up and started pacing back and forth, trying to control his emotions. "So, you're saying they threatened him. right? That's what they did!" His voice was taut. He felt like he was Charlie Brown, and Lucy had just pulled away the football. The line was quiet. "Are you still there, Cris?"

"Yeah." Cris sighed. "They were careful, but it was clear from what they were saying that Doug would be taking a huge risk by testifying. He wants to help Emma; he feels terrible for her. But he can't risk it. He just can't. I'm so sorry…" she trailed off.

Will hung up and threw the phone into the carpet. His head was exploding. *Fuck, fuck fuck.* He sat down and put his head in his hands. *Why does this happen every time we have a real defense witness? They immunize the people they want to use and then scare the defense witnesses away.* He sat there, frozen and unable to do anything for what seemed an eternity.

Finally, he looked up and stared out the window to a swirling mass of white. He slowly picked up his desk phone and called Michiko. "Hey, listen, there's been a new development. I need you to draft a letter to the judge."

He told her about the call with Cris.

"I want to make two arguments: First, you can't take the Fifth if all you're afraid of is that you might get prosecuted for perjury. There's clear caselaw on that. Second, even if he's permitted to take the Fifth, we should ask the judge to compel the government to immunize him. The law is really bad for defendants on that, so it's tricky, and he'll never do it. But we've got to make a record of the fact that Jones is only taking the Fifth because they threatened him. Someday, in the right case, the law might change."

Will put the receiver down and took a deep breath. Emma was probably back at the hotel by now. Should he call her with the news? She'd probably be pissed if he waited until morning. He looked at the phone and started reaching for it. Then he remembered that she'd been looking forward to having dinner with an old friend tonight at Le CouCou and getting her mind off the case.

He winced and put the handset back in the cradle. *She can't do anything about it anyway,* he thought. *Why ruin her evening?*

He turned back to his computer, clicked the mouse, and turned his attention back to the closing argument notes on the screen.

* * *

NOVEMBER 10, 2014

500 PEARL STREET, NEW YORK, NEW YORK

Emma trudged through the slushy sidewalks, dodging the dirt-filled puddles as best she could. She hadn't brought snow boots, and the sneakers she was wearing looked even more ridiculous with her plum dress suit, which was visible under her equally embarrassing puffy jacket. *Who knew it was going to snow this early in the city?* she thought as she quickly changed into her black pumps outside the courthouse and headed inside and up to the cafeteria.

Why Will insisted on meeting so early today, she couldn't fathom. They had plenty of time for more testimony prep after court today. The government wouldn't be resting until the end of the day or perhaps even tomorrow, and they had to call Doug first, anyway. What was so urgent?

She paid for coffee and a bottle of water and made her way toward the tables in the back where she sat down next to Will. He rubbed his hand over his cheeks and then leaned his jaw into the back of his hand and said, "Hey."

"Morning," Emma responded. She took a sip of the coffee. It was lukewarm and tasted like brown chalk, so she put it back down. "So what did we need to talk about before court?"

"Look, we got some really bad news last night. I didn't want to ruin your dinner, so I didn't call." He was having trouble making eye contact. "Doug's not testifying."

"*What*? What do you mean he's not testifying?" Emma stammered. It was a good thing she had swallowed the coffee, or it would have flown out of her mouth.

"Unfortunately, the government scared him away. The prosecutors told Cris that if he testified he told you the investigation was about Delphun and a consultant the Boston office used, they would charge him with perjury. And they also threatened to jam him up because he didn't tell Ben not to send the email. So he's taking the Fifth," Will murmured in his low, sonorous voice. He looked at the floor.

"But that's ridiculous." Emma felt her pulse quickening and her face getting hot. "How can they do that? They're threatening a witness into silence—and they say *I'm the one who obstructed justice?*" She slammed the table with her fist. "Well, that's rich, isn't it?"

Will clasped his hands together and leaned forward. "It is completely outrageous. It's infuriating. And it's dirty pool. They've got those notes. They know his testimony is true. At the very least, they know they can't charge him with perjury with those notes out there."

"Then how can they get away with this? We're in the goddam US of A, aren't we?" Emma yelled. People at a table across the room were staring at her. She lowered her voice and leaned toward Will.

He sat back and shook his head. "The truth is, the law is very unfair on this type of thing. We filed a motion asking the judge to either prohibit Doug from taking the Fifth or, at a minimum, direct the government to give him immunity so he can be compelled to testify. But judges almost always deny these kinds of motions and say only the government can decide to immunize a witness." Will paused. "And this judge in particular—" He rolled his eyes. "He's never going to believe there was improper pressure. He'll just accept whatever story they feed him."

Emma felt like she was suspended from a cliff, hanging on for dear life while the rope she was holding slowly slipped out of its precarious anchor. She tried desperately to hold back the tears starting to well up in her eyes, unable to speak.

Will put his hands on her shoulders, looked straight at her, and said, "Listen, you are going to get through this. It's riding on you now, but you can do it. You have the truth on your side. Don't give up hope."

She took a deep breath and drank some of the water as he handed her copies of the motion papers they'd filed last night. Reading them made her feel a little better, even though he said they would lose. The arguments were laid out so clearly and persuasively. How could the judge *not* see they were right? The government's response was filled with case law, but it seemed so rote. And they didn't directly respond to the most compelling points.

Was the deck really that stacked against them? *Perhaps there is a glimmer of hope, and the rope is still holding steady,* Emma thought as they headed out of the cafeteria and up to court.

Just a few short minutes later, however, the onslaught continued. And it happened so fast Emma barely had time to catch her breath.

Judge Gregory took the bench, scowling. "Please be seated. I've read the motion papers you filed last night—not sure why these couldn't have been filed earlier in the weekend, by the way, but there it is."

He shot a dirty look at the defense table. Emma gritted her teeth. How could they have acted more quickly?

The judge was reading from something. He announced: "I'm denying the mistrial motion. I don't see how the defense was prejudiced, even if these notes should have been produced earlier. The government says they're introducing them so you can make your arguments to the jury about why they're exculpatory."

Will stood up, but the judge waved his arm in a downward motion. "Sit down, Mr. Shelby. I read your letter. I know you want to recall Kuznetsov, but I don't see the point. It's just a waste of time. The government says these aren't his notes, and you already had a chance to cross-examine him about his recollection of what Mr. Jones said about the subpoena. "Now, as for Mr. Jones's testimony, based on his lawyer's proffer, it seems he has a good faith basis to assert his Fifth Amendment privilege. And I don't see how I can compel the government to immunize him. The Second Circuit cases don't permit me to do that, except in extraordinary circumstances not present here. So I'm going to deny that motion for the reasons set forth in the government's letter." He banged his gavel loudly. "Please be back by nine thirty for the jury," he snarled.

Mrs. Vappur said, "All rise."

Emma was slightly dizzy as she stood up, imagining herself in free-fall after the rope completely detached itself from the anchor. She gripped the table tightly, watched Judge Gregory saunter off, and sat down to catch her breath and steel herself for the inevitable impact.

CHAPTER 15

DEFENSE CASE (I)

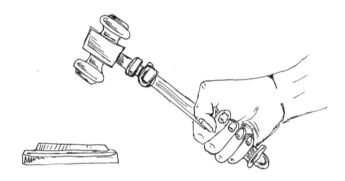

NOVEMBER 12, 2014

500 PEARL STREET, NEW YORK, NEW YORK

This was it. Showtime. The moment the whole trial had been building toward. Emma looked back at the gallery. The court-room was packed. She glanced past some of the familiar faces—the reporters covering the trial, the lawyers for Otis, and lawyers for some of the witnesses. Where was Pierre? Emma scanned the audience a bit apprehensively.

She thought back on last night's FaceTime call with Daniel and Sarah. Daniel actually stayed on the phone much longer than he had on her other calls while she was staying in the city.

He even asked a bunch of questions about the trial for the first time. "Are you sure you should testify?" he said, rubbing his forehead. "I thought criminal defendants rarely do that because it often makes things worse for them. Is your lawyer really sure the jury will believe you?"

That threw her off. *Does he think I did it?* Emma wondered. Does *he* not believe me? Or is he just curious about the process and whether the strategy makes sense?

Emma's rumination about Daniel's true feelings was cut short by the sight of Pierre's flame-red mane popping out from the masses, all the way on the right in the second row. He winked and blew her a kiss. Emma smiled at him and relaxed, just a bit.

Will stood up, walked over to the podium with his thin black binder, and said, "The defense calls Emma Simpson."

Emma felt a rush of adrenaline. She took a deep breath, rose, and walked purposefully to the witness stand. She wore a blue-gray suit—conservative, not flashy—and a slightly worn pair of navy patent leather pumps. The shoes were not her nicest pair and only had modest heels, but she chose them because they were broken in and familiar. She could not risk the newer, two-inch black ones. They looked much sharper but could inflict such excruciating pain. Anyway, a less flashy look was better. Why play into the prosecutors' depiction of hedge fund managers as greedy fat cats that ordinary people couldn't relate to?

Emma sat down and looked at the jury. *This is it*, she told herself, taking another deep breath as she heard Mrs. Vappur tell her to raise her right hand. "Do you swear to tell the truth, the whole truth, and nothing but the truth?"

"I do," Emma responded solemnly.

"Good morning, Ms. Simpson," Will said in his soothing baritone. Emma's email appeared on the large TV screen facing the jury, as well as the small monitor directly in front of her. He asked, "Is this the email you sent on March 14, 2012?

Emma looked at it and responded, "Yes."

"Why did you send it?"

Emma looked at the jury intently and said, "Ben Noguchi had sent an email to everyone in the New York office about our upcoming transition to a new computer system and new servers, reminding everyone to follow the company's document retention policy. He'd said this was a good time to organize their files before the transition. I wanted to send out an email backing up his suggestion."

The jurors looked back at her. So far, so good. At least they were paying attention.

"At the time you sent that email, did you know there was a federal grand jury investigation of Otis?" Will asked.

"No." Emma responded. "I mean, I knew there was an investigation, but I didn't know which agency was investigating, and I didn't know Otis was a target of the investigation. I just knew that a consultant our Boston office used had gotten a subpoena."

"What did you think the investigation was about?" Will said.

"I thought it was about whether this consultant was providing our Boston office with insider information about Delphun Media." Emma gazed at the jurors as she said this.

"What did that have to do, in your mind, with the Noguchi email telling New York employees to follow the document retention policy?" asked Will.

"I didn't think it had anything to do with his email, because the email was really about getting ready for the computer system upgrade, and in any case we weren't trading Delphun stock in the New York funds." Emma was looking at Will.

Shoot, I shouldn't be doing that, she thought and turned her head so she could speak directly to the jury.

"Boston managed several funds focused on media and entertainment companies, but our team was focused on other sectors—mostly health care and energy as well as some financial services companies."

"Before you sent your email on March fourteenth, did you know that the government had issued a broad subpoena calling for production of documents related to every one of Otis's hedge funds?" Will asked.

"No, I did not," Emma responded, again looking directly at the jurors.

"At the time you sent your email, had you seen the subpoena?" asked Will.

"No, I had not."

"Had anyone told you what was in the subpoena?"

"No," Emma said firmly. "All I was told was that a Boston consultant had received a subpoena about Delphun." The jurors were all looking straight at her, listening to every word. Would this last? Would they lose interest? *Stay focused. Don't think. Just tell your story,* Emma thought. She used her thumb to rub her dad's big gold wedding band, which she wore on her middle finger for good luck, as she waited for the next question.

Will shifted gears now. He had Emma tell the jury that she was born in New York City; had a BA in math and a PhD in economics, and had risen through the ranks at Otis to become head of the New York office.

Then he took her through her daily commute routine and the events of March 14, 2012. She described what she recalled about the 10:00 a.m. meeting with the New York portfolio managers and analysts.

"What, if anything, did Doug Jones say about any investigation?" he asked.

"I remember he mentioned some investigation; a consultant the Boston office used had gotten a subpoena about some Delphun trades Otis placed in media funds," Emma said.

"When Doug Jones mentioned the subpoena to the Boston consultant, did you feel worried?" Will asked.

"Objection," Ted Hardin said in a loud voice as he stood up.

"Sustained," responded Judge Gregory immediately without looking up from his computer screen. Emma was caught off guard at first but remembered Will's warning that this might happen and to just calmly wait for the next question.

"When Doug mentioned the subpoena, were you concerned?" Will inquired.

Emma started to answer, "N—"

Hardin sprang up again with another loud, "Objection!"

"Sustained," said Judge Gregory.

Will tried another tack. "Ms. Simpson, when you heard about the subpoena, did you worry about how it would affect you personally?"

"Objection!" Hardin practically screamed. This was just unbelievable. How could the judge not let her tell the jury her side of the story?

Emma gritted her teeth, trying not to show emotion, but she sensed that her face was flush with anger.

"May we have a sidebar, Judge?" asked Will, seemingly unfazed.

The judge looked up from his monitor and glanced at the clock in the back of the courtroom. "Why don't we take our afternoon break to discuss it instead?" He smiled at the jurors. "Folks, we'll take our break now so I can talk to the lawyers without wasting your time."

Everyone stood up as the jurors filed out of the courtroom. Emma tapped her fingers on her leg. Wasn't the judge going to let her explain her thought process at the time? That was the ballgame, wasn't it?

Will remained standing, calm but loaded for bear. "Your Honor, what's the objection? This case turns on Ms. Simpson's intent and state of mind. That's the whole case. And they're arguing that the subpoena freaked her out and that she sent the email because she was worried she was the target of an investigation. How can she be precluded from testifying about her reaction when she heard about the subpoena?" he said coolly.

"Your Honor, of course we don't object to the defendant testifying about her state of mind," Hardin said in his most earnest tone.

What a phony, Emma thought.

Hardin continued, "But these are leading questions. That's the nature of my objection. A simple question of 'what did you think' would be more appropriate."

"But, Judge—" Will started to say.

"He's right," Judge Gregory said, cutting Will off. Then His Honor walked off the bench.

Oh well, thought Emma. Maybe it's not that big of a deal. Everything seemed to be going well until this point, but it sounded like these objections involved a technicality. Presumably Will could rephrase the questions, and she'd be able to tell the jury why she wasn't concerned or worried when she heard about the subpoena.

A few minutes later, the judge returned, and the jury was brought back into the courtroom. "You may proceed," he said, nodding at Will.

"Ms. Simpson, at the end of the day, what did you think about what Doug Jones said about the subpoena?" Will asked.

"Objection! Objection!" Hardin bellowed, jumping up like a jack in the box.

What? Didn't he tell the judge that Will should *use the phrase "what did you think"? Wasn't that his idea of what would be "appropriate"? How could he be objecting?* Emma felt her face warming up again and reminded herself to stay calm. She took a deep breath and rubbed her dad's ring again.

"Sustained," said Judge Gregory. Emma's jaw dropped in disbelief. A couple of jurors were looking at Will. The Maddow lady was smirking. *Oh my god,* Emma thought, *they must think these questions are improper. Jesus Christ.*

Unflappable as usual, Will glanced at his binder and flipped the page. He said, "Exhibit twenty-five, please," and Emma's email appeared on the screen. Will asked: "Ms. Simpson, why did you write, 'These procedures are designed to protect the firm and its employees in case there is ever a lawsuit or regulatory inquiry. Please talk to a compliance officer if you have any questions'?"

Emma hesitated for a second, fearing the worst, but the jack—Hardin—remained in the box this time, so she fixed her blue eyes intently on the jury. "I wanted to second Ben's advice that our employees should follow the company policy," Emma explained. "And I mentioned the purpose of the policy so people would understand why it was important, not just for the computer transition, but more generally."

"And what is your understanding of the purpose of the company's document retention policy?" Will asked.

Emma explained the policy in detail, uninterrupted. The jurors all seemed to be looking directly at Emma and listening. The hardware store guy was nodding and taking notes.

"Were you thinking about the investigation when you sent this email?" Will asked.

Emma opened her mouth to answer, but Hardin jumped up again with a loud objection, which was sustained. *Not again*, she thought.

Will didn't skip a beat. "Did you have any second thoughts about sending the email?" he asked.

Once again, like a jack-in-the-box, Hardin popped out of his seat, bellowing, "Objection!"

The judge appeared to pause slightly, before saying, "Sustained."

Emma ran her hands through her hair. Why wasn't Will asking for a sidebar or trying to do anything more about these objections?

Will asked, "If the legal department had told you to preserve documents, or suspended the Otis document policy by March fourteenth, would you have sent your email?"

"Objection!" Hardin said loudly, enunciating the words slowly as *obbb—jec—sssshion*.

"Sustained," said Judge Gregory again.

Will's equanimity seemed to be dissipating a bit under the strain. "Your Honor, may we have a sidebar? This is the key issue in the case!" He started walking toward the bench.

"No," replied Judge Gregory without even looking up from his computer. "And no speaking objections, counsel," he admonished sternly.

Will turned around, put his hands in his pockets, and slowly walked back to the podium. *Keeping his cool,* thought Emma, *but he must be ready to explode.*

"Ms. Simpson, when you sent your email on your train ride home, were you thinking about the investigation Doug had mentioned during the morning staff meeting?"

"Objection." This time Hardin didn't even bother to stand up, as if the result was a foregone conclusion. He had that tell-tale smirk on his face.

"Sustained," came the answer from the judge.

Emma clenched her teeth and strained to keep her composure. She looked at the jury. Were they frustrated that information was being concealed from them? Or were they annoyed and getting the sense the defense was trying to pull one over on the court? *We've lost a few,* she thought, watching one of them looking at the audience in the gallery and another glancing at the big clock in the back of the room. *Shit.*

Will's patina of unflappability seemed to be on the verge of cracking. In an exasperated tone, he asked her, "Why did you send the email?"

"Objection. Asked and answered," said Hardin.

"No, I'll allow it," said the judge.

Finally, Emma thought, *this is my chance.* She looked at the jury and calmly explained, "I sent the email to defuse people's frustrations with the computer upgrade, which was going to cause some disruption as the new system was rolled out. I also wanted to back up my colleague and remind folks about our company policy. I wasn't thinking at all about Doug's comment about the subpoena, since I thought the investigators were looking into a consultant our Boston office used for its Delphun trades. I never would have sent the email if Doug or others in the legal department had told us to preserve any documents." The hardware store guy smiled at her and nodded again. The Maddow lady appeared to be jotting down some notes. Emma was breathing easier.

"Ms. Simpson, when you sent the email about the document retention policy on March 14, 2012, did you think you were doing anything wrong?" Will asked.

"No, not at all."

"No further questions," said Will.

Judge Gregory looked at the clock and said, "It's time to break for the day. We'll resume tomorrow morning at nine thirty."

Mrs. Vappur said, "All rise." The jurors filed out, and Emma stepped down.

It had been a long day. She was exhausted but relieved to be done, at least with the first half of her performance in this dreadful theater. She still had to walk past the reporters in the gallery, and the photographers would be waiting outside the building. She couldn't escape their shouting, or their flashbulbs, but at least she could speed by in her sensible heels to the refuge of the hotel, dinner with Pierre, and a FaceTime call with the kids. Who knew, maybe they would even have a beer or a glass of wine so she wouldn't have to think about the cross-examination ordeal ahead for the next day.

CHAPTER 16

DEFENSE CASE (II)

NOVEMBER 13, 2014

500 PEARL STREET, NEW YORK, NEW YORK

When Will walked into the courtroom the next morning, he felt a jolt of nervous energy. Was it the triple shots in the cappuccino he'd just downed? Or just the uncertainty about Emma's upcoming cross? Or both?

The trial was going pretty well so far—no thanks to the judge's blocking and tackling for the government. And she was well-prepped. He knew he had done everything he could. But still, the next act was completely out of his control. So even after all these years, he had butterflies in his stomach when the judge turned to the front table and said, "Cross-examination?"

Ted Hardin stood up, stuck out his chest, buttoned his charcoal gray suit, and swaggered toward the lectern. *He certainly acts the part well,* Will mused, *but has he ever cross-examined a defendant—or any real fact witness—before?* Most prosecutors had little to no cross-examination experience and could easily stumble in this sort of high-pressure situation. And this was Ted's first big white collar trial, after all. *But Ted is good,* Will thought as he cracked his knuckles.

"Good morning, Ms. Simpson," Hardin said.

"Good morning."

"You've worked at Otis for about twelve years, right?"

"Yes," Emma responded.

"When you started, you were a research analyst focusing on the media and entertainment sector, correct?"

"Correct. But I switched to health care several years ago."

"You've known Richard Ginsberg, the CEO of Otis, a long time?" Hardin asked.

"Yes."

"You're friends, right?"

Emma paused. "We're not close friends, but we socialize outside the office from time to time, I guess."

"Worked closely with him?"

"Sure," Emma allowed. "More directly when he was in the New York office, though. He moved to Boston a few years ago."

Ted twisted his lips. "After he moved to Boston, though, you talked frequently, right?"

"We talked from time to time, yes."

"He sometimes runs investment ideas by you, doesn't he?"

Will started tapping his fingers on his knee. *Where's this going? Is he trying to suggest she was involved in the Delphun trades?*

Emma furrowed her brow. "Sure, sometimes. But usually it's more about management issues, HR, new investors, things like that."

Hardin ran his hands through his coal-black hair. He raised his voice. "I'm not asking about what else you talk about. My question is, didn't he consult with you about media investments?"

"Sometimes he did, yes." She showed no emotion.

Good. Now's the time to move on to another topic, right? Will thought.

Hardin leaned into the podium, his steely eyes fixed on Emma. "Now, for the past several years you've managed health care funds. Is that right?"

"Yes."

"And your funds have done *very* well in the past couple of years, right?" Hardin looked at the jury for a moment.

Emma smiled slightly and looked down. "They did okay."

"You did okay for yourself, too, didn't you?"

She looked up again, not smiling anymore. "I'm not sure what you mean."

"Your compensation was based on how well your funds performed, wasn't it?"

Emma tightened her jaw. "That was part of it, yes."

"Well, that was the main part, wasn't it?" Hardin pressed.

"I got paid a salary and a bonus, and the bonus was based on my funds' performance as well as a qualitative assessment of my work managing the New York office."

"And, by the way, you made seven million dollars in 2010?"

Will glanced over at the jury warily. The hardware store guy was raising his eyebrows. *Fuck,* Will thought.

"Approximately," Emma responded.

"And ten million dollars in 2011?"

Now several of the other jurors were looking at each other and shaking their heads.

"In that range, I think," said Emma softly.

"And you stood to lose lots of income if Otis was charged with insider trading, right?"

"Uh, I never thought about that," Emma said.

"And by the way, your husband bought a Hudson Valley winery with some of your millions, didn't he?"

Now Will had steam coming out of his ears.

He shot up to his full height and projected his deep voice: "Objection."

The judge looked at the clock. "Sustained. Mr. Hardin, I think you've covered this." He smiled at Ted. "Perhaps you want to move on to your next topic?"

Why is it that even when he's sustaining my objections he has to be so nice to them, kissing their asses in front of the jury like that? Will thought, sweating a little.

"Yes, Your Honor. I was about to do that," Ted said obsequiously.

Emma's March fourteenth email flashed on the screen.

"Ms. Simpson, on March 14, 2012, you sent this email encouraging your colleagues to destroy documents, didn't you?"

Will rose. "Objection, argumentative."

"I'll allow it," the judge said.

Well, at least that gave Emma a moment to reflect on how to answer it, Will thought.

"I sent this email to assuage people's concerns about disruptions caused by the computer upgrade and to remind them to follow our—"

The judge turned to Emma and said: "The answer is yes. You have answered his question."

"I'm sorry, your Honor, I can't answer yes or no without an explanation because of the way the question was worded," Emma said firmly but politely.

"You answered the question. Let's move on," the judge said. He looked at Hardin. "Next question."

"And when you sent this email, you knew the government was investigating Otis, correct?" Hardin said.

"No, I'd been told there was an investigation of a Boston consultant—"

"Yes or no," the judge snapped. "It's a yes or no question."

Will felt as if his usually low blood pressure was through the roof. Should he object? Would the judge berate him in front of the jury? Would the jury think he was trying to protect her too much. Would this undermine her credibility?

Screw it. I need to stand up to this bullying, he thought. "Your Honor, can we approach?" he said politely.

Gregory sneered and said, "No."

"You knew when you sent the email that Otis was under federal investigation?"

"Not exactly. As I said, I was told a consultant to the Boston office was being investigated." The judge didn't interrupt this time, but that was probably because his clerk had distracted him with a note of some kind.

"And you're familiar with the Otis document retention policy?" Hardin asked.

"Yes, of course."

"In fact, you attended annual training sessions where the compliance department went over the details of the policy with Otis employees?"

"Yes, I did."

He put the policy on the screen. "The highlighted paragraph required analysts to discard any notes after the information in the notes was incorporated into a formal report, right?"

"Yes."

"But the rules are different if there is a subpoena, aren't they?" Hardin asked, his voice rising with each word.

"Well, if you know there's a subpoena *to Otis* or litigation, you're supposed to keep any documents that could be *relevant*," Emma responded.

The judge furrowed his eyebrows and peered down at Emma as if about to admonish her but said nothing.

"You're supposed to keep relevant documents under the policy, even if you don't get a specific instruction from lawyers to preserve them, right?"

"Well, again, if you *know...*"

Hardin cut her off as another page appeared on the screen. "Well, you knew, by March 2012, that this paragraph prohibited Otis employees from destroying any documents that were called for by a subpoena or requested in litigation, right?" Hardin asked.

"Yes, but I didn't even know there was a subpoena to Otis," Emma responded.

Judge Gregory's face turned red as a beet. He said sternly, "Ms. Simpson, if you are asked a yes or no question, please answer yes or no. You must only respond to the question. Do not add extra information. That's what redirect by your lawyer is for."

Will stuffed his fists in his pocket and clenched them hard. *How can he do this in front of the jury? He's basically telling them she's being evasive. And I can't even speak to her now that she is on cross.*

Hardin glanced at his binder, flipped past a few pages, and then looked up. "The document retention policy says you're not allowed to destroy documents responsive to a subpoena or litigation, correct?"

Emma bit her lip. "Yes."

"So you can't destroy documents if you know about a subpoena. Right?"

"I can't answer that yes or no," Emma said sheepishly.

Good for Emma, thought Will, *at least she realized how to deal with this.*

Then Hardin immediately asked, "Why not?"

Will smiled to himself. *Big mistake.* Hardin was grasping his pen tightly. *Bet he realized it as soon as the words were out of his mouth,* thought Will.

Emma said calmly: "Well, it depends whether the subpoena is to *Otis* and what the subpoena says, and which documents it is asking for. I didn't know there was a subpoena to Otis when I sent my email, so obviously I didn't know what documents our company was supposed to produce."

Hardin was gripping the sides of the podium. This time he paused a moment before his next question.

Too bad, thought Will. *I guess he's learned not to ask the "why" question.*

"Now, you testified on direct examination that on the morning of March fourteenth, Doug Jones told you there was a subpoena, right?" Hardin said.

"He said there was a subpoena to a consultant to the Boston office for documents about Delphun, yes."

Hardin grimaced. "But you do admit he spoke about a subpoena, right?"

"He mentioned a subpoena," Emma said.

"And you agree that he mentioned a criminal investigation by the federal government, right?"

"Yes."

"Now, you met with lawyers for Otis in May 2013, right?" Hardin asked.

"I don't recall the date, but at some point in 2013, I met with Otis's outside counsel—the lawyers representing the company for the investigation and subpoena."

"And at that time, you said you didn't know *anything* about *any* subpoena when you sent your email." Hardin paused for effect. "Right?"

"Well, I—"

Judge Gregory looked down at Emma. "Ma'am, it's yes or no."

Will could feel his veins throbbing. *C'mon, Emma, just answer. We'll deal with it on redirect,* he thought.

"Yes."

"And at that time, you said you didn't know *anything* about *any* insider-trading investigation relating to Otis when you sent your email." Hardin paused for effect again. "Isn't that right?"

Emma looked down and said in a low voice, "Yes." Some of the jurors were shaking their heads.

"And that was a *lie*, wasn't it?" Hardin's voice rose with each word, reaching crescendo as he slowly enunciated the word "lie."

Will clasped his hands together and started pressing his left thumb vigorously into his right palm. *Act like this is nothing,* he thought.

Emma clenched her teeth and took a breath. "No, it wasn't a lie."

"Well, you've just testified under oath to this jury that you *did* learn there was a subpoena *before* you sent the email, right?"

"Yes, but—" She paused. "Yes."

"Isn't it a fact that you *changed your story* after you realized the government had learned from other witnesses that Mr. Jones told you about the subpoena before you sent the email?" Hardin sneered.

This time Will couldn't stop himself from jumping up. "Objection!" he said quickly.

The judge gave Hardin a half-smile. "Sustained. You've made your point, Mr. Hardin."

"No further questions."

The judge looked at the jury. "We're going to take our lunch break now. Remember not to discuss the case. Please come back at one thirty."

* * *

At 1:30 p.m. on the dot, court was back in session.

"Any redirect, Mr. Shelby?" the judge asked.

"Briefly, Your Honor," Will said. He strode to the podium with his hands in his pockets. *Don't overdo it*, he thought. *Just a few quick points and get her off the stand.*

"Ms. Simpson, before the break, you were testifying about your meeting with Otis's outside lawyers. Do you recall that testimony?" he asked.

"Yes."

"Why did you tell those lawyers that you didn't know about any investigation or subpoena when you sent your email that mentions the document retention policy?"

Emma turned to the jury. "Well, at the time, frankly, I didn't even remember the email. When they met with me, it was the first time I'd heard anything about the investigation or subpoena, or the email, in over a year. I hadn't thought about any of it. I told the lawyers that at some point I did learn there was an investigation, which I recalled hearing was about some consultant and Delphun trades placed in Boston, but I thought that was after I sent the email."

Emma paused, took a sip of water, locked eyes with the jurors again, and continued.

"Then, after my meeting with those lawyers, I had a chance to review documents from that time period and refresh my recollection about all the events that day and the next few days. And that's when I realized that Doug spoke about the subpoena to the consultant at that meeting on the fourteenth."

"Now, you were asked some questions on cross-examination about your understanding of the document retention policy. Do you recall those questions?"

"Yes."

"Can you explain how you understood your obligations about subpoenas and litigation?"

"My understanding was that if you knew a document could be relevant to a litigation or might have to be produced because of a subpoena *to our company*, you had to preserve that document," Emma said, again looking at the jury.

"And in the past, when there was litigation or a subpoena, how did you learn about that?" Will asked.

"It only happened once or twice, but in the other cases I was told about the litigation or subpoena by someone in the legal and compliance department, *and* they sent us instructions about what types of documents to preserve."

Will leaned forward and stared intently at Emma. "Before you sent your March fourteenth email, did any of the lawyers instruct you to preserve any documents?"

"No."

"Other than what Doug Jones said at the morning meeting that day about a subpoena relating to a Boston consultant and Delphun, did anyone tell you anything else about any government investigation?"

"No."

"Ms. Simpson, when you sent your email on March fourteenth, did you think you were doing anything wrong?" Will stared into Emma's eyes.

She turned and locked eyes with the jurors. "Absolutely not. I never would have sent the email if I had known there was a subpoena to Otis and that the government was asking for documents we had in our New York office."

"No further questions."

Will closed his binder, breathed a sigh of relief, and sat down.

CHAPTER 17

JURY INSTRUCTIONS AND DELIBERATIONS

NOVEMBER 14, 2014

500 PEARL STREET, NEW YORK, NEW YORK

The sun's golden rays illuminated the gritty sidewalk for the first time all week as Will made the brisk walk from the subway to the courthouse. The air was still cold and windy, but it felt more like a vigorous breeze than a gale. Yesterday had gone well, all things considered, but this was no time to let his guard down. The draft jury instructions Judge Gregory circulated last night were a train wreck, and the charge conference was going to be contentious. He stopped along the way to pick up a triple-shot cappuccino and steel himself for the upcoming battle.

Five minutes later, he was seated at the defense table with Josh at his side, waiting for Judge Gregory to emerge from his robing room. The courtroom was largely empty for the first time in the trial, other than the few reporters diehard enough to sit through even a dry, technical discussion between the lawyers and the judge.

"They're sure to screw this up," Will whispered to Josh as he tilted his head in the direction of the gallery. "It's hard enough for the press to get even the simple things right."

"If we're lucky, maybe they'll think it's too boring to cover," Josh said as he placed down copies of their letter brief and the annotated draft charge with their objections.

Just then there was a loud knock on the robing room door. Everyone stood up, and the judge waddled over to the bench.

"Please be seated," he said. "I've got the defense letter. Let's deal with those issues first." He looked at Will. "Mr. Shelby?"

Will rose. "As our letter makes clear, Your Honor, we have two major issues with the draft jury instructions. The first one relates to what the government is required to prove as to Ms. Simpson's knowledge.

"The defense's argument, as the Court knows, is that Ms. Simpson did not intentionally do anything wrong. She knew there was *a* subpoena, but she believed it was to a consultant the Boston office worked with; she was unaware that it was even to Otis, or that it called for any documents in the New

York office. In other words, she had no idea the employees to whom she sent her email possessed any documents called for by the subpoena to Otis. We have requested an instruction requiring the jury to find that Ms. Simpson knew what she was doing was wrong, knew there was a grand jury subpoena to Otis calling for production of its documents, and knew what documents it called for when she sent her March fourteenth email.

"This is necessary because, under the caselaw, there must be a nexus between the 'persuasion' to destroy documents and a particular proceeding. The Supreme Court has held that someone who merely persuades others to shred documents under a document retention policy is not acting 'knowingly' and 'corruptly' if she does not have in mind any particular proceeding to which the documents might be material. That's the *Andersen* case."

Will paused.

"The language in Your Honor's draft charge is inconsistent with *Andersen*. It allows the jury to find corrupt intent and knowledge if Ms. Simpson knew there was an investigation, even if she didn't think investigators were requiring the production of the documents her email concerned." He continued, with emphasis, "In other words, the draft instruction allows the jury to convict even if Ms. Simpson didn't know she was doing anything wrong, but the statute requires the government to show that she was consciously engaging in wrongful conduct."

Judge Gregory narrowed his eyes. *He seems perturbed,* thought Will. *That's what you get for just mindlessly cutting and pasting from the government's requests. Maybe next time you could really read the cases, or at least have your clerk do that, and think about what's right.*

The judge looked at Ted, as always. "Government, what's your response?"

But the law wasn't really Ted's department. Annie Waters stood up.

She spoke clearly and deliberately. "Judge, the draft charge is fully consistent with the *Andersen* case. There's no need for the language the defense is requesting, which would only confuse the issues. The instruction requires proof that Ms. Simpson knew of an investigation, and that is sufficient. It's unnecessary to get into whether she specifically knew the subpoena was to Otis or whether the documents she told people to destroy were specifically called for by the subpoena. Elsewhere, the jury will be instructed that she had to 'corruptly influence' or 'endeavor to influence' the grand jury proceedings."

Will cracked his knuckles impatiently as he waited for her to finish. He felt like a caged tiger.

"That's more than ample to ensure that the jury must find consciousness of wrongdoing by this defendant," Annie continued as the judge nodded.

Annie was still standing, but Will had to pounce.

"Judge, that's simply not true," he said. "The general definition of 'corruptly' doesn't solve the legal defect, because the instructions say all the government needs to prove is that an investigation called for certain documents and that Ms. Simpson asked people to destroy those documents. Absolutely nothing in these instructions requires the jury to find that Ms. Simpson *knew* the documents she was asking people to discard were called for by the subpoena." He raised his voice. "That's the problem, and it allows the jury to convict even if she didn't know there was anything wrong with asking people to follow the company policy. It allows them to convict even if she didn't commit a crime, in other words."

Annie started to say something, but Judge Gregory cut her off. "I agree with the government. The request is denied, and the objection is overruled."

The sunshine in the window behind the judge disappeared. Dark clouds were moving in.

"Mr. Shelby, what's next?"

Will gritted his teeth and pressed his hands into the table. Should he try to keep pressing the point, telling the judge this was going to get him reversed on appeal if there was a conviction? Or would that just make the judge dig in further and screw them on the remaining dispute?

He looked down at the judge's draft language discussing credibility of witnesses and Josh's carefully crafted bullet points. He put on his best James Earl Jones voice, which always seemed to add an undertone of authority to his arguments. "Our next issue concerns the instruction about defendant's testimony. As currently worded, the instruction *eviscerates*"—he enunciated the word slowly, drawing out each syllable—"the presumption of innocence. It tells the jury that a witness who has 'an interest in the outcome' has a 'motive to testify falsely' and that the defendant's testimony should be evaluated just like 'any other witness with an interest in the outcome of the case.' But—"

The judge rolled his eyes. "Counsel, this is a fairly standard instruction in this district. And obviously defendants *do* have an interest in the outcome."

Will took a deep breath. He wanted to set the volume to eleven but managed to keep it at eight. "But, Judge, an innocent defendant does *not* have any motive to testify falsely. An *innocent* defendant has an interest in the outcome but *a motive to tell the truth.* Only a guilty defendant has a motive to lie. So this instruction basically tells the jury to presume the testifying defendant is guilty. It is plainly unconstitutional." Waters was rocking back and forth in her seat as he spoke and jumped to her feet as soon as Will stopped talking. "Your Honor, as you said, this instruction is standard, and it's perfectly appropriate. The Second Circuit has affirmed convictions in which this *exact* instruction was used. In the cases with bad instructions, the language was quite different. This instruction just says her testimony should be treated like that of any other witness with an interest in the outcome."

Judge Gregory was nodding again. "What about that, Mr. Shelby? Hasn't this standard instruction been affirmed?"

Will imagined himself in the middle of a dumpster fire screaming at the top of his lungs at the pain but composed himself and affected an air of tranquility. "No, Judge, with all due respect, that's not true." He paused for effect and said emphatically: "This instruction tells the jury the defendant has a motive to lie, plain and simple. And only a guilty defendant has that motive. So you'd be telling the jury to presume that Ms. Simpson is guilty—when the law requires the jury to presume that she's innocent."

You might just as well direct a verdict for the government! he thought but refrained from saying.

"Thank you, counsel. But I'm going to overrule your objection and leave this standard instruction as is," the judge said calmly. He looked at the clock. "Let's take a fifteen-minute break."

Ted Hardin's voice was just loud enough to overhear as he leaned close to Waters, touched her shoulder gently, and said, "Nice job. That went really well."

She shrugged her shoulders and shook his hand off. She said curtly, "Not that I had to do too much." She looked down at her feet and glanced back at Emma briefly. She mumbled, "We'll see if it holds up on appeal if we get a conviction." Then the prosecution team filed out.

Will sank into his chair, his head in his hands, unable to move. He felt Josh tapping him on the shoulder and glanced up.

"Look at the bright side," Josh said, half-smiling. "If we lose, we'll have a hell of an appeal."

"I *hate* appeals." Will couldn't help but laugh at that. Better get some more coffee and think some more about the closing argument he was giving on Monday.

When he reached the hallway he heard a loud clap of thunder. He looked out the window. Large round balls of hail were raining down.

* * *

NOVEMBER 16, 2014

PITCHER LANE, RED HOOK, NEW YORK

The sky was overcast, coated with silvery-gray clouds that created a dull, vaguely somber light. It didn't seem like it would rain, but it was clear the sun wasn't about to burst through the clouds and brighten the day. The air had that bleak feeling of cold and damp but not quite freezing—a weather limbo of sorts.

Emma pulled up the hood on her parka and gripped her soft roller bag as she looked anxiously down the empty tracks of the southbound platform of the Rhinecliff station. Where was the train? It should have been here five minutes ago.

Not that she was eager to get back to the city or her hotel room with its banal, anodyne Scandinavian furniture and urban cacophony. But she'd just as soon as get to the hotel quickly and deal with whatever lay ahead. Resolution seemed better than purgatory. At least, that's what she thought when she wasn't dwelling on what the future held in the worst-case scenario.

Pierre would leave at the crack of dawn to join her in court tomorrow. So at least she could look forward to that familiar presence to buttress her volatile emotions during the closing arguments.

The tension at brunch this morning was as tight as a frozen rubber band ready to snap at the slightest pull. After much debate about when and how to broach the subject, Pierre and Emma decided to use this meal to get Daniel and Sarah ready for some of the big changes on the horizon. Of course, there had been other talks along the way about the case and how it might affect the family's future. But she and Pierre had soft-pedaled things a bit and used the uncertainty to try and project a glass half-full outlook. And thus far, they mostly confined themselves to a storytelling mode when describing the trial, with emphasis on the high points—and scant mention of the low points.

These days the kids usually woke up late on Sundays, so family meals were a bit of a thing of the past, hormonal teenage sleep cycles being what they were. But with the trial nearing its end, Emma and Pierre had managed to cajole Daniel and Sarah into a family brunch. Emma even made her signature banana pancakes: crêpes with buttery sautéed slices of banana, topped with sugar and cinnamon and maple syrup for those so inclined. The kids hadn't asked for this favorite dish in a long time, but she loved the idea of making them (and her memories of how they enjoyed eating them when they were younger). Plus, it was one of the few things she knew how to cook since Pierre was the culinary parent.

Pierre started the conversation. "Guys, we need to talk to you about some things. We know it's been tough for you since Mom was arrested. But this trial is going to end soon, and we need to prepare for what might happen." He paused. "Of course, we all hope for the best, but we need to prepare for the worst. If things go well, we are still going to face some challenges. Things won't just go back to the way they were before this happened."

"What do you mean?" Sarah interjected. "If Mom gets acquitted, everyone will know she's innocent and that this was all a big mistake." She looked around the table. "Right?"

Daniel rolled his eyes and gave her a withering look. "Don't be so Pollyannaish, Sarah. That's not how the world works. I mean, O.J. Simpson was acquitted, right? But everyone still thinks he's guilty. He's not about to land any more acting roles."

Emma grimaced. "Is that what you think, Daniel? That I'm like O.J. Simpson? That some slick—"

Pierre jumped in to cut her off. "Calm down. Calm down. Daniel has a good point, even if the analogy is way off. Of course he doesn't think you're guilty." He shot Daniel a look, as if to say, *Now is not the time for snark.* "Sometimes what matters is perceptions. It's hard to erase people's memories about sensational headlines, even if the stories turned out to be wrong. It takes time." His jaw clenched, and he adopted a somber tone. "And look, I'm sorry to have to say this, but it's not guaranteed this jury will do the right thing. The judge has done some stuff that makes it hard for us to tell Mom's side of things, and juries are notoriously unpredictable. If we lose... Well, we've discussed this before, but..."

Daniel's face was now impassive. He interrupted Pierre. "How long would Mom be in prison? Would she get out before I start college?" His tone was no longer sarcastic but solemn.

Emma wanted Pierre to do most of the talking but couldn't help herself. She said, "We don't know; it's hard to predict. But that's possible." She gave Daniel a steely look. "That's why we have to prepare for that contingency."

Sarah had only picked at her banana pancake. She looked like she was fighting back tears, as with most conversations like this.

Pierre said, "Let's not think too much about that, but we have to be realistic about what the future may bring. Your mom has been supporting this family for a long time, but—I'm sorry to say—we really can't count on that anymore, regardless of how the trial turns out. We still have savings, but at the end of the day, I'm probably going to have to get a real job. And frankly, that will be a bit difficult. I haven't practiced law in a long time. And, I'll probably have to look for work in the city. So unfortunately, at some point we'll probably have to sell the farm and buy a smaller place, closer to the city. Which also means you'll have to go to a different school."

Now Daniel was angry. "What do you mean? Why don't you just do a long commute like Mom did?" He glared at Emma. "I'm supposed to go to a new school for my senior year? Leave my friends and my chance to finally start on the varsity basketball team?" His face was red as a beet.

Sarah's face, by contrast, had a pearl-white sheen. She stopped even pretending to eat and pushed her plate to the side. "But if Mom's acquitted, can't she work again? Even if she can't get her old job back, can't she make enough money so we don't have to move?" she said in a quavering voice, as if trying to convince herself of what she was saying.

"Maybe," said Emma. "We just don't know." She looked at Pierre for affirmation. "We will definitely try to make things work so we can stay." She knew this was overoptimistic but thought it was best to cushion the blow. This was enough for one day, especially with the outcome teetering in the balance.

Pierre tried to back her up. "Mom's right. We're just trying to prepare you *in case* we get to that point. At this point things are out of our hands, and we have to just see what happens. And I'm not even sure what the timing would be and *when* we might move. It could be less than a year, or it could be we wait until Daniel graduates. We'll just have to see."

Emma's reflections on the morning's events were cut off by the *clickety-clack* sound of the train rumbling into the station. She took a deep breath and pulled her hood down. Then she wheeled her bag toward her usual car, resigned to continue this journey despite her inability to control its final destination.

* * *

NOVEMBER 18, 2014

500 PEARL STREET, NEW YORK, NEW YORK

Lucas Jordan's back was acting up again as he slowly made his way up the courthouse steps. These past two weeks were taking their toll on him—having to trudge back and forth from 181st Street to lower Manhattan, worrying about whether he could really trust Jim to run the business, and the aggravation of having to sit through this trial. But Lucas thought he was finally seeing the light at the end of the tunnel. When he arrived at the jury room that morning, he figured today was going to be, at long last, the end of this ordeal. Yesterday was the lawyers' closing arguments, and then the jury instructions. Now, it was finally time for the jury to make its decision. Surely the deliberations would be quick—it was a simple case, after all—and he'd be back to his store tomorrow morning.

But it turned out that things were not that simple. This was shaping up to be another long week.

Jeff, an unemployed actor with long, unkempt blond hair and a goatee, was the foreperson. He started things off innocuously enough. "How about we just go around the table and everyone share their thoughts on what they think on the two counts—obstruction of a grand jury proceeding and corrupt persuasion of others to destroy documents?"

That seemed as good a place as any to start, and everyone nodded.

Elaine, a young woman who worked for the *Rachel Maddow Show*, spoke first. "Well, she's obviously guilty, in my opinion. I bet she was doing a lot of insider trading too." She rolled her eyes.

"We don't know that," said Nelson, a retired bus driver. "And she wasn't charged with that, anyway. This case is just about that email."

"I agree we should focus on the email, but it seems pretty obvious she shouldn't have sent it." This older white lady who wore baggy jeans and sneakers and carried a copy of the *Village Voice* spoke up. "She knew what she was doing. She admits she knew about the subpoena, but she sent the email anyway, telling people to destroy documents the government wanted to see." The woman shook her head. "That's what these people do. Think they run the world, these hedge fund millionaires, and can do whatever they like. She's guilty!"

"Exactly right." Elaine leaned forward and assumed a schoolmarm's tone. "This woman was making, like, ten million dollars. The last thing she wanted was for the feds to get these documents. She freaked out when she heard about the subpoena, and so she told all these people to destroy all the evidence."

Often wrong, but never in doubt, thought Lucas.

He took a deep breath and exhaled. Should he speak up yet? Nah, better to sit back and see if others would stand up to her.

The heavy-set woman with the thick Russian accent—Nina, was it?—crossed her arms and scowled at Elaine. "Ach, come on. This seem like bullshit case to me," she said. "If she so worried about investigation, why not sent email right after she hears about it instead of hours later? Wasn't even her idea. That guy Ben sent it first."

Deion, a clerk at the Metropolitan Transit Authority, jumped in. "Yeah, that's right. Plus, her story made sense. She was told the feds were looking at some consultant their Boston office worked with; she was just agreeing with Ben that people should follow the policy. She wasn't thinking about this investigation."

Jeff rubbed his fingers over his little beard slowly and looked around the room. "Even if she thought it was about some issue in Boston, the fact is, she knew there was a federal investigation, but she still told her people to throw out documents."

Several of the other jurors who hadn't spoken were nodding now.

Warming to his theme, Jeff continued: "And I don't buy her explanation, either. I bet she made up this story about Boston once she found out they could prove she knew about the subpoena. I mean, remember, the first time she was asked about this she *claimed* she didn't even know there was any subpoena when she sent the email. And that guy Mikey—he was a friend of hers—even he said they were told about a subpoena for lots of Otis documents, not just Boston documents. Simpson's obviously just changing her story to try to get out of this." He looked around the room. "And why would they make a federal case out of this if it was just some meaningless, harmless email anyway?"

Lucas had heard enough. "That happens all the time, man. People get arrested, they get stopped by the police, doesn't mean they did anything wrong. We've got to look at *the evidence*. What've they got? Nothing. Nada. This woman got, like, two hundred emails that day, she's running from one meeting to the next, she's going through her inbox on the train home, and she quickly dashes off a message agreeing with a coworker." He paused and scanned each of the faces around the room, one by one. "If you can go to prison for that, God help us all."

The Russian lady was nodding. Deion said, "Amen."

"Oh, don't be naive," Elaine said condescendingly. "That's what she wants you to believe, and she's obviously a really good actor."

"Exactly," said a guy called Luis who had been pretty quiet before. "Lady like that, all put together, with her fancy designer suits and her fake smile. Making all that money. She'd say whatever it takes to get out of this."

Lucas felt like tearing his hair out.

He was about to jump into the debate again when there was a knock on the door and everyone went quiet. The marshal came in with their lunch. Lucas looked at the clock. Had it already been three hours? *It's going to be a long afternoon,* he thought. It might be a long week.

CHAPTER 18

NOTES AND VERDICT

NOVEMBER 19, 2014

500 PEARL STREET, NEW YORK, NEW YORK

Emma sipped her coffee slowly as she gazed out the cafeteria window at the rain coating the rooftops in Chinatown—seeing but not really watching. Her copy of the *New York Times* remained folded. She picked up Michael Lewis's *The Big Short* but found herself reading the same paragraph over and over because her mind would not focus on the words on the page or retain any content. All she could think about was, *What are they talking about?* These twelve people who held her fate in their hands. And at this point, there was nothing she or her lawyers could do anymore to influence them—if there ever was at all, anyway.

Yesterday was a long day. Apart from a couple of brief trips to the courtroom, it seemed like time stood still as she spent the better part of eight hours sitting in this very spot or on one of the benches outside the courtroom—doing nothing, trying to distract herself with aimless chitchat, but mostly, just enduring this agonizing wait.

There was a flurry of activity shortly after lunch—the judge summoned everyone to the courtroom to deal with several jury notes. They wanted some key exhibits—her emails, the document retention policy, the subpoena. They asked for some testimony too—hers, Malomar's, and Mikey's. But it was impossible to read anything into these notes, other than, perhaps, that the jury was focused on the key bits of evidence. Or at least someone was, since there was no way to know which juror or jurors, or how many, even requested this information.

Maybe it was good that after a day, they were still deliberating. After all, it was a fairly short trial, and usually a quick verdict was bad for the defense—or so Will had said. But in O.J., a six-month trial, the acquittal came after a few hours. So who knew?

Emma was so wrapped up in her thoughts that she didn't notice Pierre had just arrived and kissed the top of her head.

Then she finally saw this hand being waved repeatedly in front of her eyes and looked up.

"Earth to Emma! Bonjour... *Hellooo*," he said as she flashed a winsome smile. "How are you holding up? At least they're still deliberating, right?" He gave her another kiss and sat down.

"Yeah, I guess, although it's a bit of a black box. Who knows what they're thinking?" Emma said and sighed. She looked down at her coffee. "This stuff is crap. It tastes like brown crayon." She paused. "I miss your coffee," she said as she put her hand on his.

"Well, hopefully you'll never have to taste this garbage—or anything like it—again." He pointed to her book. "Seriously? You're reading a book about how people in your industry helped tank the economy and cause a global financial crisis?" He laughed. "How about some light fiction or something? Even a murder mystery would be more distracting, no?"

Emma opened her mouth to respond, but just then Will swung by, waving his arms. "C'mon, there's another note. We need to get back to the courtroom ASAP." The couple quickly rose and followed him out.

A few minutes later, Judge Gregory took the bench, and Mrs. Vappur handed him a piece of paper. He pursed his lips and looked up. "So, we've got another note. It says: 'What does the government have to prove the defendant knew when she sent her email? Did she have to know there was a subpoena to Otis? Did she have to know that the people who received the email had documents that the subpoena to Otis was asking for?'"

Emma gritted her teeth. This was the ballgame, wasn't it?

"Counsel, any suggestions?" the judge said, looking at Ted Hardin, of course. Waters started whispering to Hardin. He shook his head and stood up to address the court. Waters gripped her forehead with her right hand and glared at Hardin, stone-faced and icy. It was like the look of Medusa about to turn someone to stone.

Hardin caught her gaze and retreated: "Your Honor, may we confer for a moment?"

"Of course," the judge said.

While the prosecutors huddled, Will and Josh spoke in low voices with Emma. "I'm going to try and push it back in our direction or, at worst, get him to repeat what he already said. Maybe it was confusing to them or ambiguous. That's better than having him clarify because he'll just say you didn't have to know the documents were relevant to the investigation."

Hardin said, "Your Honor, we think the court should simply remind the jurors of the nexus instruction it has already given. Any other option could only create confusion."

Will rose. "Your Honor, as you know, we think that instruction is incorrect and that the law requires the government to prove Ms. Simpson knew that she was asking people to destroy documents that would have been responsive to the subpoena to Otis. The court should instruct the jury that to be guilty, Ms. Simpson had to know that there was a subpoena to Otis—not just an investigation—and what Otis documents or categories of documents had been subpoenaed."

The judge was fuming, narrowing his beady eyes as he scowled at Will.

But Will wouldn't back down. "I know your Honor ruled on this issue, but I'm preserving our objection. This is a critical issue, and it's clear the jury is focused—"

"Mr. Shelby, I overruled that objection to my charge. That was my ruling. You have your objection. I will adopt the government's suggestion." Judge Gregory looked down at Mrs. Vappur. "Please bring the jury into the courtroom."

The jurors filed in. They didn't look at Emma. Was that a bad sign? She started twirling her pen. Maybe. But then again, they didn't look at the prosecutors either. She suddenly noticed the pen and put it down as she tried to read their faces while keeping her head turned toward the bench.

The judge said, "Ladies and gentlemen, I have your note. Let me remind you that, as I instructed you earlier, to find the nexus element satisfied as to either count, you must find beyond a reasonable doubt that *either*: the defendant directed the destruction of documents that were called for by *a* grand jury subpoena; *or* the defendant directed the destruction of documents that she believed could be within the scope of the grand jury's investigation. If you do not find that the government has proven one of those things beyond a reasonable doubt, you must acquit."

The jury filed out, and the judge stepped down.

Emma went back to Pierre, who looked grim. Not good. He said, "They seem focused on the right issue, but that instruction is bad. It seems like all they have to find is that the documents were called for by *a* subpoena, even if you didn't know that, or if it wasn't even to Otis. I just don't understand how that can be right. It seems to mean it doesn't matter whether you knew there was anything wrong. How can that be a crime?"

"I know, believe me. And what about the way he paused and emphasized the word 'or'?" Emma responded. She couldn't give up hope, not now, though. "But maybe it's confusing to them, and repeating it won't clarify, so…"

"Right, that's true." Pierre tried to sound more optimistic too. He put his arm around her. "C'mon, let's get some lunch now."

They headed back to the cafeteria. Another morning of deliberations, another note, but back to the seemingly endless wait for a decision on her fate.

* * *

Three hours later, Emma was again gazing out the window—this time the one outside the courtroom—as she paced the hallway and rubbed her father's ring. The weather had cleared, and Pierre had gone outside for a quick walk to get a change of scenery.

Emma's mind was racing. What if she was convicted? Would she miss Daniel's last year of high school? Would she be home for Sarah's graduation? Would Pierre have to move back to the city and get a job at a law firm? Would a law firm even hire him after all these years out of the practice? What would happen to their marriage? He'd given up his life in France for her, and she'd finally been able to help him with his dream of getting back to the wine business, but now everything was blowing up. Would she lose him too? Could their marriage survive? Ever since the arrest, she felt it was like a house of cards that could be swept away by even a little gust of wind. But now a tornado was on the horizon.

Josh came out of the courtroom where he and Will and their paralegal had been waiting. "Emma, there's another note."

Her heart started pounding. Was there a verdict? Where was Pierre? "Josh, can you text Pierre to come back? He went outside to get some air." Josh nodded, and they went inside.

A few minutes later, the judge emerged. "Counsel, we have another note." He grimaced. "It says, 'We are deadlocked and cannot agree on a verdict.'"

Emma's heart sank. What would happen now? The last thing she wanted was a hung jury and to relive this ordeal.

"What are counsel's thoughts on how to proceed? It has only been two days. It's far too early to declare a mistrial, but what about an *Allen* charge?" Emma now knew far more criminal law than she cared to think about, but this was Greek to her.

"Your Honor, may we have a moment?" Will asked. The judge nodded.

Hardin and Waters had a whispered conversation while the defense team conferred with Emma.

Will said, "An *Allen* charge is really bad. It's a coercive instruction telling the jury to keep trying to reach a verdict." He looked at Emma. "We have no idea how they're divided, but obviously it's better for us to have a hung jury than to force a verdict. *Allen* charges are never good for defendants."

Emma ran her hands through her hair. "Well, oppose it, then, obviously," she snapped. "But I don't think I can go through this again, honestly." *Anyway, what difference would it make if they opposed it?* she thought. *The judge would just do whatever the prosecutors told him to do.*

Will turned toward the judge. "Your Honor, we oppose any *Allen* charge. It's far too premature. The jury has only been deliberating a short time. We'd suggest that the court simply advise the jurors to keep deliberating and perhaps reread the part of the jury charge about the deliberative process."

"Government?" Judge Gregory asked.

The prosecutors were cocooned together, speaking in hushed tones but in an animated way, as if in a debate. Hardin had his arm on the back of Waters' chair as he whispered into her ear. But then Waters shook her head firmly, pushed her chair back to dislodge his arm, and rose to her feet.

"Your Honor, we agree with the defense," Waters said.

Emma raised her eyebrows in disbelief. Why would they agree? Maybe opposing it was the wrong call if that's what the prosecutors wanted.

Josh passed her a post-it that said, "They're probably worried that doing it now could be reversed on appeal if they win."

Great, Emma thought. *I guess they're pretty confident most of the jurors want to convict. Maybe my only hope really is that someone holds out for acquittal and hangs the jury.*

She felt paralyzed. Never in her life had she had so little control of her own fate. She stared ahead, enduring but tuning out the ritual of bringing back the jury so the judge could tell them to keep deliberating and send them back to the jury room.

Then she went back to the hallway and found Pierre, who gave her a hug and handed Emma her favorite chocolate bar, which he'd apparently picked up on his walk. A small gesture, but the sweet melty taste made her feel a little better, at least for a moment.

An hour later, after more radio silence, the jury was dismissed for the day, and Emma's life remained in its state of suspended animation.

* * *

NOVEMBER 20, 2014

The agony continued the next day. The mind-numbing wait seemed like it would never end. Emma sat for hours in the cafeteria or outside the courtroom. She had Pierre by her side, which was something.

At 4:30 p.m., there was another note. Once again, they were deadlocked. This time, however, the note was more emphatic: "We are hopelessly deadlocked. We do not think we can reach a unanimous verdict on either count or that more deliberations would change our views."

Emma huddled with her lawyers and Pierre. Will said, "I'm sorry, Emma, but I think we have to ask him to declare a mistrial."

"I just really don't think I can do this again. I don't see how. The psychological torture is probably worse than prison," Emma said.

Pierre shook his head. "Don't be ridiculous; that's crazy talk. I know another trial will be awful, but what's the alternative? Maybe if they have to stay, whoever is on your side will feel forced to give in. I mean, next week is Thanksgiving. These people probably want to be done with this. And however bad this process is, going to prison is going to be a lot worse."

"Believe me, I'm aware. I'm the one who is facing prison, not you!" Emma snapped. "Easy for you to be so calm."

"Emma, I…" he said.

Emma sighed. "Sorry, sorry. I'm just freaking out, I guess. Okay?"

When the judge returned, Will stood up. "Your Honor, at this time the defense moves for a mistrial."

Hardin said, "The government opposes a mistrial. We request an *Allen* charge."

Will objected. "Judge, this jury has been deliberating for three full days, and this is the second indication they are deadlocked. This time their note makes clear that they are irreconcilably divided. An *Allen* charge would be unduly coercive, especially with Thanksgiving coming up."

Judge Gregory leaned down and said something inaudible to Mrs. Vappur, who looked at her screen. "Maybe he's looking for a retrial date?" Josh whispered.

Apparently not. The judge said, "I'm going to give my standard *Allen* charge."

The jury was brought into the courtroom. Emma tried not to look directly at them, but she thought she saw the hardware store guy and the Russian lady looking in her direction and trying to catch her eye. What did that mean? Were they on her side? Most of the other jurors seemed to be just looking down or at the judge.

The judge turned to the jury box and said: "Once again, ladies and gentlemen, I want to thank you. We all know you worked hard, and that's very much appreciated. I understand you've been unable to reach a verdict thus far. This case has taken twelve days to try, including your deliberations, and if you fail to agree upon a verdict, the case will be left open and undecided and, like all cases, it must be disposed of at some time.

"Another trial, of course, will be costly to both sides. There is no reason to believe that the case can be tried again by either side better or more exhaustively than it has been tried before you. Any future jury will be selected in the same manner and from the same source as you all have been chosen. And there is no reason to believe that the case would be submitted to twelve men and women more conscientious, impartial, or competent to decide it, or that more or clearer evidence could be produced on behalf of either side.

"It's desirable if a verdict can be reached, but your verdict must reflect the conscientious judgment of each of the jurors. And under no circumstances must any juror yield to his or her conscientious judgment. It's normal for jurors to have differences; it's quite common. Frequently jurors, after extended discussions, may find that a point of view, which originally represented a fair and considered judgment, might well yield upon the basis of argument and upon the facts and the evidence."

Emma clenched her fists in tight balls. Why didn't Will fight harder to stop this? Wouldn't anyone fighting for her feel like the judge was pushing them to give in?

The judge lowered his voice and said something about how jurors should not change their minds "just because other jurors see things differently or just to get the case over with," but then talked more—in a louder, more emphatic voice—about unanimity and how important it was.

Emma's fists were so tight at this point that her nails were digging into her palms. The words were becoming a blur.

Finally, she heard: "Consequently, I'm going to ask you to return to the jury room once again tomorrow morning, continue your deliberations for a reasonable period, and carefully reexamine and reconsider all the evidence bearing upon the questions which have been presented to you. Thank you."

Emma's heart was pounding as the jurors filed out. Would this never end? How much longer would they be in limbo?

* * *

NOVEMBER 21, 2014

At 2:00 p.m., about an hour after the jury's lunch was typically brought to them, Emma sat on a bench outside the courtroom, staring at gray clouds moving in to cover the rooftops in Chinatown. She was trying to think about the time she'd first seen Sarah, at age eight, zoom past her and Pierre on a black mogul run at Big Sky. That girl was so fast. Boy, did that piss off Daniel! But then Will crashed into her reminiscence with a tap on the shoulder.

"Another note?" she asked. She had butterflies in her stomach.

He nodded, and they went inside.

The judge was on the bench, laughing at something his law clerk apparently had said. As soon as the prosecution team arrived, he said, "We have a verdict."

Emma's heart stopped. After all the waiting and longing for this to end, she was suddenly overwhelmed with terror. Goosebumps covered her flesh, and she crossed her arms to try to warm up.

The jurors filed in. Their faces were expressionless and stone cold. None of them would look at her. *Oh my god*, thought Emma. She felt like the butterflies had all been slaughtered and that their corpses were rotting in her intestines.

Judge Gregory said, "Mr. Foreman, I'm told by your note that you have a verdict. Please hand it to the clerk."

Mrs. Vappur took an envelope and handed it to the judge. He reviewed it and handed it back to her. "Please publish the verdict."

Mrs. Vappur read, "United States versus Emma Simpson, verdict form. Count One, obstruction of a grand jury proceeding. How do you find Emma Simpson? Guilty. Count

Two, witness tampering. How do you find Emma Simpson? Guilty."

Emma heard, "Please poll the jury," and then, fainter, "Juror Number one, is this your verdict?" and then undecipherable words, and then ringing in her ears. The words got more and more muffled, and she started to feel dizzier and dizzier.

Then, just as the last voice said, "Yes," she fell to the ground, and everything went black.

PART FIVE

EPILOGUE

CHAPTER 19

ANOTHER DAY IN THE LIFE OF EMMA SIMPSON

RED HOOK, NEW YORK

MARCH 14, 2015

Emma's fitful slumber was jarred by Pink Floyd's "Comfortably Numb," which shattered the silence in the bedroom. She rolled over and reached for Pierre, but all she felt was a pillow. She rolled the other way and hit the off button. Seven o'clock. Half an hour until they had to hit the road. She quickly showered, dressed, and headed to the kitchen.

Pierre poured her a cup of coffee and handed her a plate bearing freshly made multi-grain waffles with blueberries and maple syrup. She breathed in the rich aroma emanating from her cup and drank and ate wordlessly. When would she enjoy such a delicious meal again?

"Should I wake up the kids?" Pierre asked.

"No, I'll just kiss them goodbye on the way out. It will upset them more if we wake them up and make them wait around until we're ready to go," Emma said, looking down at her feet where Ghost and Dyer were huddled, snoozing comfortably. She ate much slower than usual, trying to savor every last bite.

Twenty minutes later, she went upstairs. Sarah hugged her so tightly it seemed she would never let go. She finally broke free and approached Daniel's room. She turned the knob quietly and peeked inside. He looked like he was asleep. She started to shut the door when she heard him groggily say, "Mom, aren't you going to say goodbye?" She tiptoed over to the bed and kissed his forehead. "Love you," he mumbled. "Sorry I've been such a jerk." She hugged him tightly, trying to fight back her tears, and then quickly slipped out.

After those doleful goodbyes, Emma took a last look at Pitcher Lane, just as the sun broke through the pinkish-purplish sky. Then they were on the road to Danbury, Connecticut, where Emma was to spend the next twenty-two months of her life. Emma thought grimly about how, during that time, she would be living in a box and would only see Pierre in the confines of a monitored visiting room and only speak to him on monitored phone calls. She knew she should make the most of the drive. It was the last chance for them to have a meaningful interaction for a long time. But she wasn't really in the mood for talking.

"Do you want to listen to music? Or should we listen to that Reacher book?" she said.

"Whatever you prefer," he said.

Then Emma remembered that the drive wasn't long enough to finish the book and that she wouldn't be able to listen to the rest of it with Pierre since she would be in the prison. "Those books are fun to listen to, but let's wait until the next trip. Why don't we play some music instead?" she said as she gazed out the window, watching the sun light up the brown winter fields and wondering when that might be.

A little over an hour later, the car arrived at the entrance to the prison camp. Pierre parked, and they both got out of the car. "Don't forget to send all those books," Emma said. "You have to send them through Amazon, or they won't accept them for me. And send me a small chess set too."

"I know. I know," Pierre said. He clasped her in a tight embrace.

"And make sure to send me pictures from Sarah's hockey tournament next weekend," Emma said, choking back tears.

Pierre put his hand on her face and kissed her cheek gently. "Listen, this is going to fly by. Whatever happens with the appeal, you're going to be home soon." He whispered, "I love you so much."

"I love you too." Emma didn't want to let go. They stood there for a while, locked together as one. Finally, she released him. "I guess I have to go in there now," she said softly.

He kissed her again. "We'll see you next weekend."

"Okay," she said and forced herself to turn away. As she walked into the building, she looked back and saw Pierre standing in front of the car, watching her. She studied him for a moment and then went inside.

Minutes later, a surly guard whisked her into an office where she was photographed, fingerprinted, and lectured about a long list of rules. Then she was directed into another room.

"Strip," said a female correction officer. Emma blushed and looked down at the ground. She took off her clothes and was searched—everywhere. Was this really necessary? Did they really think she had a shank or heroin up her butt? And wasn't this a prison camp for low-level offenders, anyhow?

She was tempted to make a wisecrack but sucked in her pride and bit her tongue.

Then the woman handed her an orange jumpsuit, slip-on sneakers, and some bedding. She put on the prison garb and was shuttled off for more paperwork and then into a large dormitory-style room to her assigned bed.

Emma made the bed slowly. It must have been lunchtime since no one else was around. As the emptiness of the drab room began to slowly sink in, Emma took a deep breath and sat on the bed.

Then she took out the memo her appellate lawyer, Colin Barr, had sent. "We have strong arguments that the district court committed two errors in the jury instructions, either of which could lead to reversal of your convictions," it began. Emma reread the fifteen-page memo for what must have been the tenth time. Then she tucked it away under her bed, trying to expel any hope from her mind. *Remember, life is like a box of chocolates. You never know what you're going to get.* Would there be light at the end of this long tunnel, after all?

Or just more darkness?

AUTHOR'S NOTE

———

Imagine you're a banker doing your job the way anyone in your industry would. One day, you're going to work and then home to your family; the next, you're arrested for fraud, but for doing something that wasn't fraud and wasn't illegal.

I had a case just like that, and it not only keeps me up at night but also inspired this book. As a criminal defense lawyer, I wanted to write a book that would call attention to the fact that innocent people can be and are prosecuted. I've handled a number of cases in which something unfair or wrong happened to a client accused of a crime.

Often justice ultimately prevails, but only after years of uncertainty. If you're very lucky, you might be acquitted after a trial, or if you are wrongfully convicted, you might win an appeal. Even in these scenarios, the harm to the person's life is incalculable and irreparable. As one public figure famously said after being acquitted of fraud charges, "What office do I go to to get my reputation back?"[1] Sometimes the system can fail, and you can go to prison even if you have ample

---

1   Raab, Selwyn, "Donovan Cleared of Fraud Charges by Jury in Bronx," *New York Times*, May 26, 1987.

resources and good lawyers. It can happen to anyone. And if it happens to those who have resources, it happens even more to those who do not.

My banker client, for instance, was wrongfully convicted of federal fraud, and the unfairness in his case was extreme. First, a jury convicted him for standard business practices that were not illegal but erroneously labeled "fraud." Then an appellate court affirmed his conviction under a totally different, but also incorrect, legal theory. On top of that, when my client testified at his trial, the judge instructed the jury that he had "an interest in the outcome" of the case that gave him "a motive to lie." It is true that every criminal defendant has "an interest in the outcome." But an innocent person has a motive *to tell the truth;* only a guilty person has a motive to lie. The instruction eviscerated the presumption of innocence, which is one of the most important principles of the American justice system. In fact, the appellate court pointed this out in two other cases decided around the same time, and it granted new trials to two similarly situated defendants. But in my case, that court refused to give my client any relief despite this instruction, which effectively told the jury to disregard his testimony.

The criminal justice system can go wrong for many reasons. Sometimes jurors come to a case with conscious or unconscious biases that prevent them from evaluating evidence at face value. There are all sorts of these prejudices—they can be based on race, gender, national origin, religion, LGBTQ+ status, or more subtle biases relating to wealth, lack of wealth, a defendant's profession (e.g., bankers and politicians are held in low esteem by many these days), and many other characteristics. Also, jury service is inconvenient and can be time-consuming. In criminal cases, any verdict must be unanimous. Sometimes jurors with firmly held convictions can have their will overborne by the majority out of impatience and wanting to get back to their jobs and normal lives.

In other cases, witness testimony can present problems. As more and more psychological studies show, eyewitness testimony is unreliable, and people's memories can be inaccurate and malleable. Sometimes witnesses shade the truth or simply lie. They may be motivated to lie because they have their own criminal problems (or potential criminal exposure) and think the only way out is to help the prosecutors or for various other reasons.

Trial judges sometimes (usually unconsciously) bend over backward to help the government in small ways. And appellate courts, for their part, are not perfect either. For good reasons, they are neither permitted nor equipped to revisit jury verdicts from scratch or to second-guess trial judges' fact-intensive judgments. Sometimes they may be concerned about the possibility of setting a guilty person free and might be reluctant to correct a significant legal error in the person's trial.

Some might wonder how an innocent person could be charged in the first place. It's not that prosecutors are bad people or that it's common for them to go after people without a good reason. I'm sure most wrongful prosecutions are brought by well-intentioned professionals who believe, for one reason or another, that the defendant has committed a crime. Sometimes they just make a mistake or exercise bad judgment. Sometimes they might believe "the end justifies the means" and bend ethics rules for what they think is a good cause.

In sum, while our justice system is one of the best in the world, the scales are weighted toward the prosecution, and injustices can happen. I wanted to tell that story from the perspective of a relatable defendant—someone who might remind readers of themselves, or a friend, family member, or neighbor. I also wanted to use a fictional story to make the ideas more accessible and to avoid the technical complexities of my banker client's actual case.

Although the story is fiction, when the book shows interactions among prosecutors during an investigation, how they interview witnesses, and what happens in a courtroom, the scenes draw on my experience as a prosecutor and as a defense lawyer. The book is set in my hometown, New York City, and a town in upstate New York—Red Hook, in the Hudson Valley. The characters are entirely fictional but are intended to represent a realistic picture of how lawyers, judges, clients and other players in the system behave and react to the types of events portrayed in the book.

The alleged crime in the book is "obstruction of justice." It seemed easier to create a compelling fictional story about that sort of charge, rather than about the complex financial transactions most white collar cases concern. In addition, it is very common for prosecutors to resort to such "process" crimes when they lack evidence to prove a "real" underlying crime.

My hope is that the book will educate people about some realities of the criminal justice system. If more people understand the system, they'll be more skeptical of how they view evidence if they are called upon to serve as jurors, and perhaps that will help produce fairer trials. In addition, I hope the book will inspire my readers to work toward criminal justice reform, in whatever small ways they can. And perhaps it will also help people understand that sometimes the solution to a problem isn't to imprison people.

Some industries may need reform or more regulation, but if so, lawmakers should enact new rules and regulations.

We shouldn't react to every new problem by throwing people in jail for doing things that were legal when they did them.

ACKNOWLEDGMENTS

I could not have written and published this book without the encouragement and assistance of many others.

Thanks to my daughter Emily, who encouraged me to write this book and connected me with Eric Koester and his Book Creator Institute, without whom this would not have been possible; to my husband Jonathan, who put up with me during this process and provided input and a sounding board along the way; to Natasha Shapiro, who provided insightful comments on an early draft; and to my parents, Jacqueline and Isaac Shapiro, and my sons, Matthew and Andrew, for all their love and support.

I am deeply grateful to Peter Hutt for his constructive comments and helpful advice on an earlier draft of the manuscript; to Peter Ackerman, for his encouragement and feedback and (along with Joanne Leedom Ackerman) incredibly generous support for this project; to Cynthia Arato, for her moral support and counsel on intellectual property issues; to Anne Healy, for her comments; and to Erin Petersen, whose captivating illustrations enabled me to add a visual element to my story.

I am also incredibly humbled and deeply thankful for the support of the many other friends, family members, and others who have helped spread the word about this project and placed their faith in me by preordering the book, including David Scheper, Robert Davis, Tom Hentoff, John Cline, David Parse, Mark Kaiser, Justin Singer and Tortoise Investment Management, Kevin Downey, Joan McPhee, Barry Berke, Eric Olney, Jeremy Temkin, Christine Chung, Sean Hecker, John J. Kenney, Michael Margolies, David Toscano, Douglas Winthrop, Adriaen M. Morse, Jr., Tobias Shapiro, Tai Park, Kathleen Cassidy, Paul Schoeman, Nathaniel Marmur, Victor Bach, Thomas Arena, Alan Scheiner, Charles Stillman, James Darrow, Jamie Levitt, Sean Nuttall, Eugene Volokh, Dan O'Neill, Jillian Berman, Alex Ellerson, David Schiffer, Lynn Neils, Jennifer Segal, Gary Pressley, Patricia Pileggi, Robinson Holloway, Noreen Kelly, Maria Galeno, Isabelle Kirshner, Silvia Serpe, John Schachter, Nathan Seltzer, Tara Kazak, Pamela Talese, Casey Vitiello, Marc Isserles, Will Binkley, Scott Iseman, Frank Wohl, Margie Berman, Lauren Capaccio, Karl Motey, Daniel Brown, Elizabeth Kennedy, Yotam Barkai, Bernard Ozarowski, Sarah Mueller, David Einhorn, Eric Brown, Justine Harris, Andrea Weiss, Margery Feinzig, Rhett Millsaps, Cathryn Carlson, Lisa Ferrari, Bob Gage, Sandra Hauser, Joshua Stein, Fabien Thayamballi, Tom Brown, Charles Clayman, Roland Riopelle, Steven M. Cohen, Evan Barr, Susan Bozorgi, William Reckler, Joanna C. Hendon, David Lat, Celeste Koeleveld, Theresa Trzaskoma, Eugenia Bullock, Michael J. Grudberg, Daniel M. Gitner, Zoe Bullock, Sarah Coyne, Richard Shapiro, Janna Bullock, Rebecca Ricigliano, Jacob Wolf, Alex Bodell, Linda Imes, Susan E. Brune, Lisa Cahill, Cathy Goodman, Amy Walsh, Carrie Cohen, Suzanne Jaffe Bloom, Doug Jensen,

Paulina Hatzipetrakos, Jonathan Shapse, Amy Millard, Jacqueline Wolff, Walter Loughlin, David Brodsky, Sara V. Morgan, Amelia Hritz, Brian Jacobs, Sharon L. McCarthy, Lynne Morgan, Cara Brown McCormick, Virginia W. Sigety, Helen Gredd, Nathan Buchok, Daniel Peris, Lynn Oberlander, Donna Goggin Patel, Marion Bachrach, Kirk Benjamin, Jennifer Freitag, Diana Davis Parker, Nancy Kestenbaum, Nicole Friedlander, Marjorie Peerce, Julian Brod, Ted Sampsell-Jones, Holly Kulka, Annie Epstein, Wendy Rogovin, and Luke Langenbach.

Last but not least, thanks to all my amazing editors, especially Cassandra Caswell-Stirling and Olivia Bearden, and to Brian Bies and all the other talented and dedicated people at New Degree Press for their assistance and support throughout the publishing process.

Printed in Great Britain
by Amazon

81369384R00159